Fake Marriage Planning Inc.

A Philly Series Romcom: Book 1

Anne Hagan

Jug Run Press

Contents

Chapter 1 - Iva

♥

A Saturday Afternoon in Mid-June
Iva

Iva adjusted the bride's veil, ensuring it fell perfectly over her face. Her practiced hands moved with grace and confidence as she stepped back to admire the results. The white fabric cascaded down, creating an ethereal effect that brought tears to the bride's eyes.

"Thank you so much, Iva," the bride gushed, reaching out for a hug. "Everything is perfect."

"Of course, Sarah." Iva offered a warm smile and squeezed the bride's hand reassuringly. "This is your day, and we'll make sure it's everything you've dreamed of."

As co-owner of 'Celebrate with Style' with her best friend Jon, Iva had built a reputation as one of the city's most sought-after wedding planners. The duo's impeccable taste and attention to detail had made them the go-to team for couples, hoping for a memorable celebration.

"Knock, knock," Jon called out, entering the room with a handful of delicate flowers. "The flower fairy has arrived."

"About time, Jon!" Iva teased, stepping back to admire her handiwork on Sarah's veil.

"Darling, perfection takes time." He winked, then after moving the bride's veil aside temporarily, Jon effortlessly rearranged the flowers he'd brought in her hair, adding the perfect finishing touch. He caught Iva's eye, and she gave him an approving nod.

When he finished, he straightened the veil again. "There, now you look like a vision straight out of a fairytale."

"Thanks, Jon." Iva smiled, grateful for his help.

"Thank you both so much," Sarah said, touched by their efforts. "You two are magicians."

"Only the best for our brides," Iva replied with a smile, masking the ache in her heart.

Iva and Jon had been inseparable since their college days, where they first discovered their shared passion for event planning as part of the planning committee for the college's gay/straight student alliance. Their bond only grew stronger when they took the leap and started their own business together after graduation.

Monday Evening

Iva and Jon sat in their brightly lit office, working late, poring over the event plans for multiple upcoming events. The scent of coffee filled the air as they juggled budgets, timelines, and clients' ever-changing demands.

Iva's eyes flicked between her phone and the screen, multitasking as usual. "Ugh, these flowers still won't be in season," she groaned and rubbed her eyes. "Why can't people just stick to seasonal flowers?"

"Because they think we're miracle workers," Jon replied as he scrolled through an old-fashioned Rolodex of his contacts.

"Do you think our supplier can get them from a greenhouse somewhere else? The bride has her heart set on them."

"Better. I've got a guy who runs a greenhouse," Jon said, already dialing the number. He held his phone to his ear, waiting for a response. "Hey, it's Jon. We need rainbow tulips for a wedding in less than two weeks. Can you make it happen?"

As Jon spoke on the phone, Iva let her mind wander for a moment. She thought about her recent breakup with Terri, and how the silence of her brownstone had become deafening since they'd parted ways. The loneliness, with only her inaccurately named aloof cat Cuddles to keep her company, gnawed at her, leaving her yearning for something more profound–true love.

"Thanks, you're a lifesaver," Jon said, hanging up the phone. He turned to Iva, noticing her distant expression. "You okay?"

"Fine," she lied, forcing a smile. "Just tired."

"Me too," Jon admitted. "But hey, at least we can say we're successful workaholics, right?"

"True," Iva chuckled. "It's just... sometimes I wonder if there's more to life than this. You know, like having someone special to share it all with like you and so many of our clients have found."

Jon's expression softened. "Iva, honey, I know things have been hard for you since the breakup. And I'm here for you, always. But don't lose sight of what we've built together. What you've achieved is incredible."

"Thanks, Jon," Iva said, touched by his support. "I just wish I could find someone who understands me as well as you do."

"Give it time," Jon advised, placing a reassuring hand on her shoulder. "You deserve the best, and I know you'll find it."

"Since you sound so sure, maybe you should start planning my fairytale wedding," she joked, trying to shake off her melancholy.

"First, we need to find you a prince or princess charming," Jon laughed. "And trust me, when we do, it'll be a wedding for the ages."

With a nod of appreciation, Iva turned back to their work, determined to continue pushing herself in both her professional and personal life. She knew that true love was out there somewhere, and she wouldn't stop searching until she found it. But for now, she focused on what she did best–creating unforgettable weddings and celebrations alongside her best friend.

Nearly Two Weeks Later

Iva's heels clicked on the marble floor, the sound echoing through the empty reception hall as she and Jon inspected the final touches of their latest wedding creation. A canopy of fairy lights twinkled from the delicate tulle swags draped overhead, casting a warm glow on the tables adorned with rainbow tulip centerpieces.

"Wow, we outdid ourselves this time," Jon said, admiring their work. His phone buzzed on top of the piano, the screen lighting up with a message from Nathan. "Miss you," it read, accompanied by a heart emoji.

"Aw, Nathan misses me," Jon said, grinning at Iva. "But he knows how important our work is."

"You know you don't have to be here all the time, right? You should spend more time with Nathan."

"Hey, I'm here because I want to be," he assured her. "Besides, what kind of best friend would I be if I didn't help you find your own happiness?"

Iva smiled gratefully. "You're truly the best, you know that?"

"Of course I do," he teased, nudging her playfully. "And I know it's tough, especially with Terri gone, but you'll find your person, too. Maybe it's time to get back out there, yeah?"

Iva shifted uncomfortably under Jon's gaze. "I don't know, Jon. Dating again sounds exhausting."

"Come on, Iva. There's an entire world of princes and princesses just waiting to sweep you off your feet," Jon teased, nudging her playfully.

"Fine, fine," Iva relented, trying to steer the conversation away from her love life. "Thanks," Iva said, touched by his unwavering support. As they continued to admire their handiwork, she couldn't help but feel a pang of loneliness. The beauty of the weddings they planned only seemed to magnify her own longing for true love.

Sensing she was still uneasy, Jon asked, "Have you given any thought at all to dating again?"

"Maybe," Iva admitted, her gaze fixed on a stunning flower arrangement. "I don't know. It's hard to find someone who understands my passion for this job and having most of my Friday nights and all day and evening Saturday of nearly every weekend tied up like you do."

"Trust me, they're out there. Your fairy tale ending is waiting for you, too, I promise," Jon reassured her, placing a comforting hand on her shoulder. "You just have to be open to finding it."

"Maybe," Iva murmured, her gaze drifting to the dance floor and she briefly imagined tomorrow's happy couple as they danced together as spouses for the first time. "It's just... I've put so much of myself into this job, this business. I don't even know where to start."

"Start with what makes you happy, outside of work," Jon suggested. "Go on dates when you can. Try new things. Let yourself be vulnerable."

"Vulnerable? I don't know about all of that," she replied. She shifted the conversation away from herself. "For now, let's just focus on making this the best wedding yet."

"Deal," he agreed. "And, let's not forget, we beat out Married with Magic for this wedding. That right there should cheer you up."

"Jon, we didn't compete for it. You know how I feel about chasing engagement announcements."

He held up his hands in mock surrender. "I know! I know! I'm just saying Married with Magic went after them, and they picked us anyway."

"Because we're the best—"

"Ha! Eat our dust, M-W-M!" Jon exclaimed, striking a triumphant pose. "But I know, it's not a competition." He winked at her, and they both laughed.

"Right," she agreed, rolling her eyes. "It's about making dreams come true."

Laughing, Iva gave up. "I was about to say, in an understated way the couple obviously recognized."

Jon waved her off.

Iva stared at the stack of fabric swatches, her thoughts swimming with indecision. Usually, she could mix and match colors effortlessly, but today, she found herself second-guessing every choice. The lingering heartache from her breakup with Terri had seeped into her work, leaving her vulnerable and questioning everything.

Memories consumed her thoughts. The way Terri used to laugh, the smell of her perfume, the warmth of their intertwined hands. Iva sighed heavily, lost in the past.

"Hey," Jon said softly, walking up to her. "You've been staring at those swatches for fifteen minutes now."

"Have I?" Iva asked, blinking away her distraction. She glanced down at the samples and sighed. "I just can't seem to decide."

"Is this about Terri?" he inquired gently.

"Maybe," Iva admitted. "I didn't think it would still affect me so much."

"Breakups are tough, especially when you were together for as long as you and Terri were." Jon placed a reassuring hand on her arm. "But you'll get through it. We always do, right?"

"Right," she agreed, trying to muster a smile. "I just don't want it to keep interfering with my work. We've got this anniversary party to plan."

"Take your time. Everyone has off days."

"Thanks, Jon."

"Anytime," he replied, giving her arm a light squeeze. "Now, what do you think of this combination?" He pointed to a set of swatches featuring blush pink and gold accents.

"Actually, that's perfect," Iva said, the fog of uncertainty dissipating as she refocused on her work. "It's elegant and timeless."

"See, girl? You've still got it!"

She chuckled but stopped when she heard the bell over the door in the outer shop jingle. She asked instead, "You didn't schedule someone in and forget to tell me again, did you?"

He shook his head. "Not me. I learned my lesson that time you made me pick out bridesmaid dresses with the Bridezilla from..."

"Jon! Shh! There's someone out there."

A man in his mid-twenties wearing jeans, a t-shirt, and a Phillies baseball cap was waiting up front. His face was as smooth as a teenage boy's face, and his eyes were wide with a pang of anxiety in them.

"Looks nervous," Jon whispered as they approached him. "Bet he's fake."

Iva gave Jon an elbow nudge. "All grooms *are* nervous when they first come in here."

She walked toward the younger man, saying, "Welcome to Celebrate With Style. I'm Iva. How can I help you?"

The man took off his hat and ran a hand through his hair. His voice wavered as he replied, "Am I supposed to give you my name? I'm not sure how this is supposed to work."

"Told you," Jon muttered loud enough for her to hear.

"Is there a password or something?" the man asked. "My buddy told me about you," he said as he looked over his shoulder at the door behind him.

Iva swallowed back the ethics that were bubbling to the surface of her mind and took pity on him. "Fake wedding, or fake marriage?" she asked in a whisper.

The guy looked confused. "What's the difference?"

Jon let out a, "Whoo boy! This one is all yours."

Iva schooled her face and tried to ignore Jon's antics. She got closer to the customer and explained. "A fake wedding is where we do things to make it look like you're preparing to get married, but you don't actually go through with a ceremony. You call it off, let's say. A fake marriage...well, that's usually a marriage of convenience. You have a real wedding; as small or as big as you want it, but you're marrying someone for what we'll call business reasons."

"I sort of need both."

"Pardon?"

"Uh, yeah," he stammered, running a hand through his hair. "I need a fake wedding. Like, the whole thing–engagement, ceremony, everything. I need it to look real so I can get my inheritance."

"I'm sorry." Iva shook her head. "I'm afraid we can't help you with that." *As far as deceit goes, that's a bridge too far for me.*

The man's face fell. "I was afraid of that."

Jon, who never left the room, sidled back over to them. "Can I ask; why you need a fake wedding?"

Iva cringed internally. She'd learned it was better not to ask. The answers, since she and Jon did their first marriage of convenience a few of years before, if they weren't about an inheritance, were often heartbreaking. For their LGBT customers, they often involved acceptance in a conservative family or workplace. She had long justified what they sometimes did for couples by telling herself the relationships she helped to create may not have been real, but she was still helping people get to their own joy and happiness.

The man was saying, "My grandfather died a few years ago. Now my grandmother is really sick. Everything goes to me when she passes, but only if I'm married."

Even though she'd heard it all before, bile rose in Iva's throat. They'd done several marriages of convenience for the same purpose; each couple officially getting married. She knew a few of the couples had found love together and remained together. This man, though...this man! He wanted them to help him commit an all-out fraud in front of who knew how many witnesses, all for money.

"Sorry sweetie," Jon started, while Iva shook herself out of her reverie. "We're not in the business of helping people commit fraud. Plus, orange really isn't my color."

"Look," the guy said defensively, "it's not like I'm trying to scam anyone. I just need it to look legit for a little while."

Iva had to know. She asked, "What does the woman you're going to pretend to marry think about this plan?"

He scrunched his forehead. "There isn't one. I'm not seeing anybody. I thought—"

Jon shook his head. "We don't provide the fiancée. That's our motto."

As the door slammed shut behind the would-be customer, Iva gave Jon a light slap on the back of the shoulder. Her expression was a mixture of amusement and disbelief. "Since when do we have a motto?"

Jon played dumb. "What?"

"We don't provide the fiancée?"

"Well, it's true."

Iva threw her hands up. "I guess I can't argue with that logic."

Jon started laughing, but stopped himself and asked in a sober tone, "Did he seem honest to you?"

"Clueless, but not dishonest," Iva said, but she narrowed her eyes in suspicion. "Why do you ask?"

"I think he was a ringer for our not so good buddy over there at Married Without The Magic.'

"Jon! Be nice."

"I am."

She ignored his purposeful mangling of the name of their closest competitor and asked instead, "What makes you think that?"

"That he wasn't honest? Just a feeling. You should have asked him who his buddy was who referred him to us, especially after he popped out that he didn't even have a fiancée."

"I think he was legitimate. Misguided, but legitimate."

"Well, we'll never know, now."

Chapter 2 - Cheyenne

♥

C heyenne stared at one of her computer screens without really seeing it. The freelance assignment was due in a few days, but she was having a hard time concentrating.

She flipped through her interview notes on the second screen. The city's leaders had made a statement, to send a message to the rest of the world--that they would not be bullied by the recent wave of violent crimes, but she was still puzzled about what the actual root cause of the steep rise in crime was. She was so stumped; she knew she should go back to the drawing board and talk to more people, but there just wasn't enough time.

The music blaring from the street outside her townhouse had grown so loud that it penetrated even her noise canceling headphones. She ripped them off her head, wanting to scream in frustration. Deep down, she knew she should go out and join the party and meet some people. The only thing keeping her indoors was fear of her deadline.

She walked to the windows that faced the street in the living room of her rented brownstone and looked at the scene going on outside. The sun was sinking behind the horizon, casting long rays of orange and red light across the sky. It didn't matter to the partiers below. The party had been raging for hours and they were still going strong.

She'd only lived in the neighborhood a few months, but she'd seen the flyers everywhere for the 31st annual block party. Her heart ached for a sense of community and belonging, something she hadn't had in a long time. She tried to shake it off.

Should have worked at a coffee shop today. It would have been quieter.

A call interrupted her reverie. She walked back to her desk and glanced down at her phone. *Mom*. She didn't answer.

She knew what her mother wanted. Ruth Moore wanted her youngest daughter to come to the lake for the monthly summer bash. She wasn't going. Too much chaos. She missed her sister and her kiddos, but she didn't miss the barbed comments from her father, and her mother's constant prying into her personal life.

She tried to resume her work, but the music still blared. Her stomach was growling, and she really craved some human contact now that her family was on her mind.

"Alright, block party, you win," she muttered to herself as she stood up, stretching her legs. She saved and backed up her work, then shut everything down.

In the kitchen, she grabbed a twelve pack of Diet Pepsi and a pack of Diet Dr. Pepper from her stash. *If you can't beat them, join them. May as well eat.*

She dropped the twelve packs off at a donation table as her contribution to the party and got in line for the food table.

Her stomach continued protesting the lack of nutrients while she waited in a short line. It was late in the day. She had not eaten lunch and breakfast felt like a lifetime ago. The scent of grilling meat and the sight of piles of corn on the cob and sliced watermelon made her mouth water. She was hungry enough to eat anything available, but she knew better than to gorge herself. A once daily diet soda was one of her few indulgences. An otherwise healthy diet was important to her. When her job took her on the road, she often faced multiple threats. Fight or flight was a choice she'd had to make more often than she cared to admit.

Cheyenne held her plate slightly aloft as she weaved her way through the groups of chatting neighbors sitting in bag chairs and the gangs of marauding kids running about with water guns. She opted to sit on the steps of her own stoop rather than squeeze herself in at one of the picnic tables scattered about along the block.

As she took a seat, she nodded to her neighbors on the left who sat on their front stoop a lot. She saw the older couple often as she came and went and had stopped to chat with them a few times about their day. They enjoyed people watching, and Cheyenne thought it sounded like a good plan for lunch while she ate.

She took a bite of her grilled chicken and sighed with pleasure. The flavor was out of this world. It had been so long since she had tasted anything so delicious. The juice dripped down her chin. She mopped it up with her fingers and licked it off, savoring every drop.

"How is it?" her elderly neighbor, Al, called out.

She patted a napkin to her mouth and called back to him. "It's delicious."

Gina piped up. "It's all about the marinade; my Al's secret recipe."

Cheyenne thought about the rows of chicken on the massive grill that had been built in the street for the occasion. "You're kidding, right? That must have taken days to marinade all of that."

"Nah," he said. "We have a crew. We did it all yesterday and put it in the coolers in the bodega on the corner."

Cheyenne nodded her appreciation and waved, but her attention had been drawn to a woman sitting by the gay man that lived with his significant other in the brownstone on the other side of her rental. She didn't know his name, only that he was a pretentious sort. But the woman. The woman. *Wow!*

Cheyenne couldn't take her eyes off her. She was stunning–long, dark hair cascading down her back, full lips, and a curvy figure that made Cheyenne's mouth water. She was wearing a form-fitting white dress that hugged every curve, and Cheyenne couldn't help but imagine what it would be like to run her hands along the woman's body.

As if sensing someone was looking at her, the woman turned her head and caught Cheyenne staring. Cheyenne quickly looked away, embarrassed. When she looked back, the woman was staring off into space, lost from the world despite the crowd and the noise all about her.

"Who is she?" Cheyenne wondered, feeling a sudden urge to meet the intriguing stranger. Pushing aside her usual reservations, she decided it was time for introductions.

"Here goes nothing," she murmured, rising from her seat and heading towards the captivating woman who did not know that her life was about to change.

Chapter 3 - Block Party

Iva felt like the neighborhood planning committee always picked the hottest Saturday of the summer for the annual barbecue block party. She was there, but she wasn't feeling very festive. She was melancholic as she thought about her parents and their involvement in planning the event in years past, and distracted because Terri was coming over to collect the last of her things.

Jon sat next to her on an outdoor couch, fanning himself with a folding fan he bought at the bodega on the corner. He stopped fanning briefly and said, "I'm glad we don't have any events booked this weekend or next. It's just too hot."

Iva was truly miserable. First, there was the heat. Then she sighed and admitted to her friend, "Since it's the first time off we've had in a while, I'm expecting Terri to show up and get the last of her things sometime this evening."

"Oh, sweetie." Jon offered her sympathy and was about to say something else when another woman came over to them and kissed Iva firmly on the lips.

Startled, Iva blinked as the newcomer pulled away, looking both apologetic and exhilarated.

"Forgive me for being so forward," the stranger said as she pulled back, "but you looked like you needed something. A pick-me up, a change of mindset. Something. Forgive me?"

Jon said, "What you just did to my friend could be called assault."

Iva was taken aback at first herself, but she was also intrigued. She ignored her best friend. Turning to the newcomer, a playful glint in her eyes, she asked, "Could I have another one since I wasn't prepared for the first one?"

"Really?" Cheyenne hesitated, but obliged, leaning in for a second kiss. This time, Iva responded with greater enthusiasm, their lips moving in sync.

As they broke the kiss, Cheyenne stepped back. "I'm sorry," she whispered again before disappearing into the crowd.

"Who was that?" Iva asked Jon. She knew Jon knew everyone.

"I think her name is Cheyenne, but don't quote me."

"That's a hard name to just guess at."

"I may have gone and peeked at her mailbox."

Iva refrained from rolling her eyes. "Typical. You'll never change, Mr. Nosy Pants."

"Nobody has called me that since junior high." He gave her a light fist bump on the shoulder. "Now, do you want to know more or not?"

"You're going to tell me no matter what I say."

"Damn right. She moved in next door to Nathan and me the other way, about two months ago. She seems nice, or she did until now, at least, but I don't really know her. It doesn't seem like she's there much."

Iva quirked an eyebrow. "Seems nice? She just kissed me, out of the blue, twice."

"Ha, you rhymed!"

"What?"

"Nice. Twice. They rhyme."

"Jon, focus here."

"Admit it, the second time wasn't out of the blue. You asked for that."

"It was worth it," Iva admitted. *Whoops. I said that out loud.*

"Was it, now? Do tell."

She was saved from answering by Jon's partner Nathan, collecting him and dragging him off somewhere.

Twenty minutes later, Iva trundled down to her own brownstone—one she inherited from her deceased parents after a freak accident five years before. It was just down the block from the one Jon and Nathan had bought and done extensive renovations on a couple of years later, when she let the guys know it was about to go on the market.

Terri had been pestering her to come and get some things she'd left behind. Iva spotter her ex up the street, near the food tables, with an unknown man in tow and watched as she greeted several of Iva's neighbors as if she still lived on the block.

Disgusted, feeling pangs of anger and hurt, Iva left to wait where she didn't have to watch her ex glad-handing and flirting with people.

Cheyenne sat on her stoop questioning herself and what she could have possibly been thinking a few minutes after the kiss...kisses, when she noticed the target of her lips first eyeballing a man and a woman, then get up from her seat and leave.

When the couple followed shortly behind the target of her unsolicited - the first time - affection, Cheyenne forgot all caution as she forgot all caution and made another snap decision. She followed discreetly behind the two newcomers and watched from a distance when they seemed to part ways. The woman walked up to a brownstone and entered it without him.

When the man turned and wandered back toward the thick of the party, curiosity got the better of her. Cheyenne tiptoed up to the open door and listened in on the conversation inside. She could hear someone inside angrily yelling at someone else about withholding her things for so long.

"Come on, Iva," a voice said, "You're not still mad, are you?"

"Just get your things and leave," a voice Cheyenne recognized said.

Peering through the open door, Cheyenne could hear the new woman's voice rising in anger. "You've been keeping my stuff to make things difficult for me! You're so petty, Iva!"

Cheyenne knew that this must be why the kiss of the target of her affection felt hollow, and without thinking twice about it, she knocked on the door frame of the open door. When the voice she recognized answered, Cheyenne made up a lie to save the woman from the awkward situation she'd obviously been dreading.

Stepping just inside, she called out, "Hey there. Sorry to bother you. Do you have that ketchup you said we could have?"

Iva looked stricken for a moment, but then she beckoned Cheyenne to follow her to the kitchen where she grabbed ketchup out of her fridge. She thanked Cheyenne in a whisper for being there yet again when she was about to lose her mind.

Cheyenne whispered back that she would return the ketchup later and took her leave before she did anything else that was impulsive and potentially grounds for a restraining order.

###

Iva

Cheyenne smiled at Iva and thanked her for both not slapping her for being so forward and not getting mad when she stepped in where she knew she probably shouldn't. She handed the ketchup back to Iva. "We really didn't need this. Let's just say the party won't be running out of it soon."

"No? Who knew?" Iva grinned to soften the sarcasm.

"I'm Cheyenne," the other woman said, fidgeting slightly. "I don't want to take up any more of your time, but I wanted to come by and apologize for my impulsiveness earlier, at the party. It's just that... I don't know, you caught my eye and I couldn't help myself."

"Iva. And, apology accepted," Iva said, her dark eyes twinkling with amusement. "Besides, it was a pleasant distraction from everything else going on today."

"You're welcome to come in. I could use some company after all that drama."

Cheyenne accepted the invitation and followed Iva into her living room.

"I'll just take this to the kitchen," Iva said, holding up the ketchup. "Make yourself comfortable. Can I get you anything?"

Patting her stomach and shaking her head at the same time, Cheyenne declined. "I couldn't, possibly."

Iva tried to mimic her motions, but couldn't, since she was holding the condiment bottle. "That's some coordination you have there," she called back over her shoulder to her new acquaintance.

"Thanks. Lots of practice," Cheyenne said, as she took a seat on the sofa. "I can't speak the language of every country I've been in, but some things are universal."

"Oh, you travel a lot?" Iva thought about what Jon told her. She thought, as she returned from the kitchen, there was something about this woman that intrigued her, and she found herself eager to unravel the mystery.

Cheyenne was nodding. "Freelance journalism and investigative reporting. A little ghostwriting too," Cheyenne answered with a shrug. "It's not as glamorous as it sounds to people, but it pays the bills and lets me travel. How about you?"

Iva took a seat on the other end of the sofa as she responded, "I'm an event planner." She watched in amazement as Cuddles wandered over to Cheyenne and rubbed against her bare legs. Cuddles hated Terri and avoided her the whole time she lived in the brownstone.

Cheyenne reached down with one hand and scratched the cat along his back as she pointed with the other hand toward the window and the street level a story below. "You plan all of that?"

"Heavens no! None of it. There's a whole committee for that. Elections, officers...you name it. My folks though, they were involved in all of it and in the Christmas Walk for years." Her tone sobered. "This was their place. I lost them to a freak car accident about five years ago now. They loved bringing people together." Iva glanced toward the windows. "On days like this, I really miss them."

"Wow, I'm so sorry. And, if you don't mind my saying, they must have been young. You don't look that old."

"Mom was 51. Dad was 53."

"Way too young."

Iva changed the subject. "Are you from around here? I don't recall ever seeing you before."

"I grew up in the suburbs. Got away as soon as I could."

"But you came back?"

"Sort of. I needed a steady landing place between gigs that was close to an international airport. Philly is as good as anywhere else, and a lot less expensive than say, New York or L.A., plus I can get to New York quickly from here if I need to."

"What brought you to this neighborhood?"

"Trying to get rid of me?"

"No," Iva said. "Just curious."

"My job keeps me on the go, so having a place close to my family, but not too close to them, works well for me. Plus, it's a great area–lots of interesting people and things happening." She gave Iva a megawatt grin.

"Like impulsive kisses at block parties?" Iva teased, raising an eyebrow.

"Exactly," Cheyenne laughed, her eyes crinkling with amusement. "Never a dull moment around here."

As the laughter died down, the sound of the party outside faded. Cheyenne glanced at her watch and sighed. "I should probably get going. But hey, if you ever need someone to get you out of a jam again, just give me a call."

"Thank you," Iva said sincerely, walking her to the door. "And speaking of getting out of jams, if I can ever help you--"

"Well..."

"What?"

"Since you're offering, would you be interested in going to my family's monthly picnic tomorrow? It's at my parent's lake house north of the city, on an inlet to Beltzville Lake." She hesitated. "It would be a long day. It's a bit of a drive, so only if you're not busy, of course."

"And you want me to go with you?"

Cheyenne spread her hands. "They're constantly on me, when I can make it to one at all, to meet someone, and now I have. I mean, it doesn't mean we're a couple or anything, but we have *met*. If you're available, that is. No plans or anything. No events?"

Iva hesitated for a moment, weighing the pros and cons in her mind. It wasn't like her to make impulsive decisions–especially with matters of the heart. But then, hadn't Terri been a calculated risk? And look how that had turned out. Maybe it was time for a change of pace. "Sure," she said finally, surprising herself with the decisiveness in her voice. "Why not? I don't have any plans tomorrow, and it sounds like fun."

"Great!" Cheyenne's eyes sparkled with genuine excitement, and Iva couldn't help but feel a little thrill run down her spine at the sight. "Just be prepared for some chaos. My family can be... overwhelming."

"Event planner, remember? I can handle it."

"You may live to regret that. It's a crazy large family. Think something like a reunion. Come to think of it, maybe I should have told you all of that first."

"I'm sure it will be fine."

"Well, okay then. We eat at noon, but the festivities usually start by 11:00. Should I pick you up here at, say, 10:00?"

"Are we driving?"

"Yes, and Sunday traffic isn't that bad going out, but the summer traffic back into the city might be a monster."

"It's okay. Fine, really. Should I bring anything?"

Cheyenne spread her hands. "Honestly, I don't even know." She ran a hand through her shock of dusty brown hair. "Let me call my sister and see. If we need to, I'll take care of it."

The event planner in Iva screamed a warning that it was odd Cheyenne didn't know something so basic, but she pushed the thought aside. "Okay. I guess, I'll see you at 10:00, then."

"Casual," Cheyenne said. "Shorts are fine, and bring a swimming suit if you think take a dip in the lake."

Iva felt a shiver run down her spine at the thought of being thrown into such a chaotic situation, but she pushed it away. After all, hadn't she been craving something new and exciting? This might be just what she needed to shake off the lingering melancholy from her breakup with Terri.

As they walked towards the door, Iva couldn't help but notice the way Cheyenne's hips swayed with each step, and she felt a familiar warmth spread through her. It had been a while since she'd allowed herself to feel attracted to someone, and even though she was nervous about meeting Cheyenne's family, she couldn't deny the thrill of anticipation that coursed through her veins.

As she closed the door behind Cheyenne and leaned against it, Iva's heart raced with a mix of anticipation and nerves. The thought of meeting Cheyenne's large, boisterous family as her date was intimidating, but she couldn't deny the thrill of spending more time with the intriguing woman who had literally swept her off her feet.

Shaking off her doubts, Iva focused on the task at hand - what to wear for the family gathering. She rummaged through her closet, pulling out various outfits and holding them up in front of the mirror. Each one seemed to scream 'event planner,' not 'casual barbecue guest.'

"Come on, Iva," she muttered to herself, tossing aside another blouse that seemed better suited for a wedding than a family gathering. "You've got this. It's just a barbecue."

Suddenly, inspiration struck. She pulled out a pair of comfortable denim shorts and a soft, well-worn T-shirt that read 'I put the "elusive" in "influencer." *Perfect*.

She skipped the swimming suit. *Too much pressure*.

With her outfit sorted, Iva spent the rest of the evening tidying her place and chatting with Jon on the phone. Their conversation was filled with laughter and playful banter, with Jon teasing her about her unexpected date. Despite her lighthearted demeanor, Iva couldn't shake the nagging feeling that she was diving headfirst into something far more complicated than a simple family barbecue.

"Relax, Iva," Jon reassured her, picking up on her apprehension. "You've got this. Just be yourself and everything will be fine."

"Thanks, Jon," she replied, managing a small smile. "I appreciate the pep talk."

"Anytime, babe." He blew her a mock kiss through the phone before hanging up.

As Iva settled into bed that night, her thoughts raced with images of what the following day might hold. She couldn't help but wonder if she was making a mistake by agreeing to attend the family gathering on such short notice. The whole situation seemed too good to be true - a beautiful, intriguing woman appearing out of nowhere and whisking her away to a family gathering? It was like a scene from a rom-com, and Iva half expected someone to yell "cut" at any moment.

But as sleep finally claimed her, one thought remained clear in her mind - no matter what happened tomorrow, she'd face it head-on, just like she always did.

Chapter 4 - Picnic

♥

A Summer Sunday
Cheyenne

A warm breeze tousled Iva's long black hair, and she squinted against the bright morning sun as she stepped outside and walked toward her.

Cheyenne leaned against her car, watching, trying to look effortlessly cool in a pair of shorts and a plaid button-down shirt that accentuated her tomboyish figure. "I thought you might have had second thoughts," she said to the beauty before her.

"I admit, I'm a little nervous, meeting the parents and all already." They both chuckled at that.

Iva shifted in her seat to face her as they set off. "Your family must really love these barbecues. I mean, once a month is pretty impressive."

"Ha, yeah," Cheyenne replied with a crooked smile. "It's kind of a big deal for them. They love having everyone together. But fair warning: my family can be a bit... overwhelming."

"Overwhelming how?" Iva wondered aloud, her curiosity piqued. "That's the second time you've alluded to that."

"Have you ever seen one of those nature documentaries where hundreds of birds descend on a single tree? That's my family in a nutshell," Cheyenne joked, casting Iva a playful glance.

Iva laughed, her nerves momentarily forgotten. "Well, I've always been good with birds."

As they continued their drive, the bustling cityscape gradually gave way to picturesque countryside dotted with charming country homes and then homes with a decidedly more lakeside feel. Iva couldn't help but feel a sense of calm wash over her as they neared their destination.

"Almost there," Cheyenne announced, turning onto a gravel driveway that led to a beautiful lake house with a sprawling lawn. The place was already teeming with activity - children running around, adults chatting animatedly, and the mouthwatering scent of barbecuing food wafting through the air.

"Ready?" Cheyenne asked, her brown eyes searching Iva's face for any signs of hesitation.

"Let's do this," Iva replied, trying to project an air of confidence she didn't quite feel. She took a deep breath, mentally preparing herself for whatever chaos awaited her.

As they stepped out of the car and onto the sun-drenched lawn, Cheyenne felt a strange mix of excitement and trepidation.

Iva's head swiveled, taking in the sights around them as they walked toward the house - a well-manicured lawn and bunting on the porch where people were setting up tables laden with food for the picnic.

Picnic tables were set up out on the side lawn, close to the lake. A handful of children scampered about among them. Many were in swimming suits, but they seemed to have more interest in the food that was coming from the house than in the lake only 50 yards away.

"I'm so nervous," Cheyenne said.

"Why? Are you worried about what everyone will think of me?" Iva asked, trying to make light of the situation.

Cheyenne smiled. "Yeah, a little."

"Don't worry. I won't embarrass you, I promise," Iva said.

Cheyenne felt bad. "That wasn't what I meant. It's just that, well I've been out to my family for a long time, but—"

"You rarely bring your dates here?"

"I rarely have dates."

"Is that right? So, what's wrong with you?"

"What? Nothing, I—"

Iva laughed. "Easy there, sport. I'm an adult. I can handle your family and whatever they throw at me."

"It won't be bad. At least, I hope it won't."

They reached the house and were greeted immediately by a woman with a kind face and a mane of unruly red hair who hurried down from the porch when she spotted them. Cheyenne introduced her as her sister, Daks, short for Dakota. "Mom was on a western kick over the years we were born."

"Nice to meet you, Iva," Daks said. "I've heard absolutely nothing about you." She gave Cheyenne a look as she said, "She's been holding out on me."

Iva jumped to Cheyenne's defense. "Really, she hasn't. We haven't known each other long." *Not even twenty-four hours.*

Daks raised an eyebrow. "And she brought you out here? Good luck!"

"That's the second time in two minutes I've heard that sort of thing." She turned on Cheyenne. "What aren't you telling me?"

A swarm of kids surrounded them then, each vying loudly for Cheyenne's attention. She introduced them as fast as she could to Iva, who seemed utterly charmed by the chaos.

Two tow-headed boys latched onto Cheyenne's legs, chanting "Aunt Cheyenne" on a loop.

Cheyenne ruffled their hair. "What is it, monsters?"

The older boy pointed at Iva. "Who's she?"

"Manners, mister," Daks said. "We don't point."

"This is Iva, my friend. Be nice." Cheyenne looked at Iva. "I apologize in advance for anything inappropriate they might say."

Iva waved her off. "Don't worry about it. I'm an expert in wrangling unruly kids." She stuck out her hand to the boys. "Hi, I'm Iva. What's your name?"

The younger boy hid behind his brother, but the older one eyed Iva curiously. "I'm Billy. Wanna play kickball?"

"Maybe later, buddy. Right now, I'm just meeting everyone." Iva glanced at Cheyenne and winked. "But I'm always up for a game."

Cheyenne blinked, stunned. Her date was actually charming her way into the family. Maybe this day wouldn't end in disaster after all.

"No kickball until after lunch, otherwise we'll never get you to sit and eat," Daks told the kids. "Now, off with you."

Daks turned back to Iva. "He's going to hold you to that."

Iva grinned. "I'm fine with that, I think. As long as they go easy on me. It's been a while."

Cheyenne extracted herself from the remaining tangle and linked her arm through Iva's. "Come on, let's get something to drink. I could use a beer after that welcoming committee."

Iva laughed as they moved toward the porch. "They seem like a lively bunch. Your sister has her hands full."

"You have no idea." Cheyenne glanced back over to where Daks was corralling her own kids and a few stray cousins. "Want to know how many nieces and nephews I have?"

"Sure, hit me."

"Eleven, and those are just Dak's four kids and the ones on my dad's side of the family. From his brother and two sisters."

Iva's eyes widened. "Wow. That's...a lot."

"Tell me about it. They're all here, from what I can tell, and they're all obsessed with their Aunt Cheyenne." Cheyenne grabbed two bottles of beer from a cooler and offered one to Iva. They moved to one end of the porch and stood facing the lake.

"Sorry about springing all the kiddos you like that. I should've given you a heads up about the chaos you were walking into."

"You actually did. Several, and one vivid one. Remember the whole birds to the tree thing?" Iva took a long swig of her beer and sighed. "Honestly, it's kind of nice. Reminds me of my family get-togethers. We're a rambunctious bunch too."

"Oh, really?" Cheyenne perked up, interested in learning more about Iva's family. It seemed they had more in common than she realized.

"Yep. I'm an only child, but my mom and dad both came from big, Italian clans. Family events usually descend into chaos, but that's how we show our love." Iva smiled wistfully. "We fight and bicker, but, we've always got each other's backs."

The screen door creaked open, drawing Cheyenne's attention. Her father came outside, looked around, and spotted her. He called her over.

Cheyenne tugged Iva's hand as she mumbled out of the corner of her mouth, "May as well get this over with." She introduced Iva to her ultra-conservative father, Thomas Moore, as a new friend, she'd recently met.

"Your date?"

"Not a date. We just met. You're always telling me, you and mom, to bring a guest, so I did."

"But you might be dating soon?" a woman asked as she exited the house and approached them.

"You always knew how to make an entrance," Cheyenne said to her mother. She turned to Iva. "This is my mother, Ruth Moore."

Iva shook Ruth's hand, feeling a bit out of place in her shorts and t-shirt next to the older woman who wore a Liz Claiborne sundress and a pair of sandals that cost more than her annual SEPTA pass to get around the city and surrounds when she wasn't driving her events van. "It's nice to meet you, Mrs. Moore."

"Please, call me Ruth," she said with a smile.

Thomas cleared his throat and addressed Iva. "I'm sorry to be rude, but I must ask, what exactly are your intentions with my daughter?"

"Now, Thomas," Ruth began.

Thomas Moore put up a hand to stay his spouse.

To Cheyenne, Iva looked stricken. She couldn't blame her, but she couldn't form words to reply to the rude overture, either.

Iva got out a nervous sounding, "I-I'm not sure what you mean."

"Cheyenne has always had trouble settling down." Thomas's mouth twisted, as if the words left a bitter taste. "She has spent far too much time gallivanting around the world for that job of hers. It's high time she found a nice...partner, settled down, and started a family."

Iva bit back a scathing retort, clenching her hands at her sides. How dare he speak about Cheyenne as if she was some unruly child in need of discipline?

"With all due respect, sir," she said through gritted teeth. "Cheyenne is a grown woman perfectly capable of making her own life decisions. And whether she settles down is entirely up to her."

Thomas's eyebrows shot up in surprise, clearly unused to being spoken to in such a manner. But Iva refused to back down, meeting his judgmental stare with one of her own.

After a long, tense moment, he sighed. "You have a point, I suppose." He eyed her contemplatively. "Very well, Ms. Romano. You seem to genuinely care for Cheyenne, and that is all I can ask for." A wry smile tugged at his lips. "She has always had a rebellious streak. Perhaps you are just the woman to tame her, if anyone ever could."

Cheyenne rolled her eyes. "Dad, come on! Lighten up."

"Sorry," she whispered to Iva after she tugged her away.

Cheyenne and Iva wandered off the porch and over to the picnic tables where the rest of the family was gathering for lunch. As Cheyenne made her rounds, introducing Iva to aunts, uncles, and more cousins than she could count, she saw Iva took it all in stride. She seemed to have let the overstepping of her father roll off her. She mingled easily, asking questions and sharing details about her own big, crazy family. By the time they sat down to eat, as far away from where her father normally sat as possible, Iva seemed completely at ease and was joking around with Cheyenne's family as if she'd known them for years.

Cheyenne breathed a sigh of relief and dug into the feast of burgers, hot dogs, salads, and desserts spread before them. Her family could be a lot to handle, but so far, other than her father, they were on their best behavior and seemed to genuinely like Iva.

As Cheyenne finished the last bite of a juicy burger, a tug on her sleeve made her turn. Billy, her favorite nephew, was peering up at her with wide, imploring eyes.

"You promised you'd play kickball with us after lunch! We're all done," he whined. Several of his cousins chimed in, too.

Cheyenne wiped her mouth with a napkin and nodded. "You're half right." She pointed at Iva. "She said she would, and I think she'd be a great addition to your team, but I'll play too."

"The more the merrier!" Billy cheered. "But, you have to be on the other team because we're going to beat you." He grabbed Iva's hand and tugged her along toward the makeshift kickball field, barely giving her a chance to wipe her own mouth on her napkin, let alone giving her a chance to protest.

Cheyenne snickered, happy to see Iva so easily accepted into the fold, even if it was at the insistence of a gang of kids. Her family could be intimidating, especially her father, but maybe this day wouldn't end in disaster after all. In fact, she thought, it's turning out to be pretty great.

Chapter 5 - Kickball

♥

Iva

Iva let herself be dragged along by the enthusiastic Billy, shooting a helpless look over her shoulder at Cheyenne.

When they reached the field, Billy pointed at Iva and shouted to a group of kids, "She's on our team!"

A few of the kids peered at Iva with open curiosity. A young girl with pigtails wrinkled her nose and asked, "Who're you?"

Iva waved, suddenly feeling self-conscious in her shorts and t-shirt. The way they were all dressed, even the ones in their swimming gear, told her these kids were clearly from money, probably went to private schools and had tutors and personal trainers. What would they think of her?

She shook off the insecure thoughts. She was here as Cheyenne's date, and if Cheyenne's family liked her, that's all that mattered.

"I'm Iva, Cheyenne's friend. She invited me to join your game." Iva introduced herself to the girl with a smile.

"Do you know how to play kickball?" the pigtailed girl asked critically. "Because if you don't, you'll just mess up our whole team!"

"Now, now, be nice," Daks chided gently as she joined them on the field, hands on her hips. She shot Iva an apologetic look. "Don't mind her, she's just competitive. You'll do great!"

Iva smiled, relieved to have an ally. "Thanks, but it's been a long time since I played kickball." She looked back at her teammates. "You'll have to go easy on me!"

"We will," Billy promised earnestly. "Right, guys?"

A chorus of reluctant agreements followed. Iva grinned, already fond of the rambunctious group. She turned to look back at Daks and saw her setting up a chair to watch. "Not playing?"

"Oh, no," Daks said. "I'm here to cheer you on and watch Cheyenne."

"Why cheer her on, and not me?" Cheyenne complained from the grouping she'd been relegated to with the other team.

Daks chuckled. "The kids have been plotting their revenge on you for a game they say you won by cheating two years ago ever since you called me last night."

"I never cheat!"

"Save it for the kids," Daks said.

"Oh, it's on." Cheyenne turned to Iva. "Get ready!"

"I'm ready. Bring it on!"

As Billy's team prepared to take the field, Iva noticed Cheyenne watching from the sidelines, a soft smile on her face. Her heart did a little flip. It was nice to know Cheyenne approved of how she was interacting with her family. Now she just had to prove she had game—literally!

She tried to remember the rules of kickball. She knew it was like baseball, but with a big rubber playground ball instead of a baseball, and you kicked instead of batting. Beyond that, she wasn't sure. She prayed she didn't mess up.

When it was Billy's team's turn to kick, Billy went first, kicking a pop fly into the outfield that was easily caught for an out. The next child also kicked pop fly that was caught.

Then it was Iva's turn. She took a deep breath and eyed the ball, trying to psych herself up. Don't overthink it, she told herself. Just kick the ball!

She ran up and gave the ball a solid kick with the inside of her foot. It sailed into the outfield, rolling fast along the grass. Iva raced to first base, heart pounding, as the outfielders scrambled after the ball.

She slid into second base, panting, as the ball made its way to the infield.

"Safe!"

A cheer went up from her team.

Iva looked over to find Cheyenne applauding, a huge grin on her face. Warmth flooded Iva, chasing away the last of her nerves. She was going to enjoy every minute of this game—and the rest of the day with Cheyenne.

"Nice kick!" Daks told her after she scored. Daks gave her a high five. "Told you you'd do great!"

Iva laughed, brushing dirt off her shorts as she stood up. "Beginner's luck!"

"We'll see about that," Cheyenne called from the field, her eyes gleaming with challenge. "When we're up again, you better watch out!"

"Bring it on!" Iva shot back, her competitive spirit rising. This was turning out to be her kind of family function, after all.

Cheyenne stepped up to kick and smacked the ball hard. It sailed between first and second base, rolling fast. Cheyenne raced around the bases at top speed, sliding into home plate just as the ball came in, raising a cloud of dust.

"Safe!" the uncle umpiring the game called. Cheyenne popped up, grinning.

"Show off," Iva called to her.

"Just giving you a run for your money," Cheyenne replied. "Don't want you getting too cocky on your first time out."

"In your dreams," Iva shot back.

When it was Billy's turn to kick again, he kicked the ball with all his might. It flew high over Cheyenne's head in left field. She raced after it, getting under it just in time to catch it for the out.

"Lucky catch!" Iva yelled.

"All skill," Cheyenne called as she jogged back toward third base with the ball. Less loudly, to Iva who was waiting on the sideline for her turn to kick, she said, "Admit it, you're having the time of your life."

Iva grinned. "Maybe."

"Thought so." Cheyenne bumped her shoulder. "My competitive spirit is rubbing off on you."

"We'll see who's more competitive," Iva warned. "I'm just getting warmed up!"

Cheyenne's eyes gleamed. "Promises, promises!"

Iva laughed, happiness bubbling up inside her. What had started as a stressful day was turning into one of the best she'd had in ages. All thanks to a woman who had crashed into her life and was now refusing to leave.

Not that Iva minded one bit.

Iva made a diving catch that ended the game for her team with a win. Billy clapped her on the back as they left the field. "You can be on my team next time!"

She beamed at the boy, while she masked the burning pain shooting from her right ankle, up to her calf.

She tried not to limp as they walked back to the picnic tables, but Cheyenne caught it.

"You okay?" she asked.

"Yeah. I twisted my ankle, I think, on that last dive. I'll be fine, but no more kickball for me today."

"Chey," Daks said, "go get some ice. I'll get her settled on the porch, in the shade, and get that ankle propped up."

When Cheyenne did as she was commanded, Daks turned back to her and leaned in close. "She worries too much, that one. But it's nice to see she cares so much already."

Iva felt her cheeks heat at the implication. "We're just friends."

"For now," Daks said, a knowing gleam in her eye. She patted Iva's arm. "For now."

Cheyenne returned to the porch with her mother, an icepack, and bottled water for everyone.

Iva took the water and gulped it gratefully while Cheyenne's mother fussed over her ankle and arranged the ice just so.

"Mom's a nurse," Cheyenne said as she took a seat next to Iva on a fancy outdoor settee.

"Was," Ruth said. "Well, I keep my license current, but I only tend to my family."

"I'm fine, Mrs. Moore, really," Iva said.

"It's no trouble." She took a seat next in a chair adjacent to Iva. "I apologize for Thomas," she said without preamble. "I used to stay quiet about his blather. I don't anymore."

Cheyenne shot Iva a look, but Iva wasn't about to interject an opinion anyway.

"He's very conservative. Tried to raise his girls that way, too." Ruth Moore looked at Daks and Cheyenne and then back at her. "Fortunately, they didn't buy into all that crazy nonsense. I still stay out of it."

Daks, who had seated herself adjacent to Cheyenne, and Cheyenne both guffawed, loudly.

"Now girls, you know I don't believe all that stuff."

"True," Cheyenne said. "But that's not why we're having coughing fits over here."

Daks said, "You don't stay out of anything, Mother."

"Now tell me," Ruth leveled an eye on Iva, "how is one supposed to find out anything if she doesn't ask questions?"

Iva turned toward Cheyenne and shrugged. "She has a point."

"I've been watching you two today," Ruth said. "You've got something special, Iva. Anyone who can make Cheyenne smile like that is welcome in my home."

Iva saw Cheyenne's cheeks flush, though she didn't protest her mother's words. Iva's heart did a little flip, warmth blooming in her chest. Still, she hesitated, biting her lip. "I appreciate that, Mrs. Moore, but Cheyenne and I are really just friends. I wouldn't want there to be any misunderstandings."

"Please, call me Ruth." She waved a hand, unconcerned. "Thomas can be overprotective, but don't you worry. As long as you treat Cheyenne well and make her happy, that's all that matters to me."

Iva nodded, some of the tension easing from her shoulders. At least she had one ally here. "Then you have my word."

"Wonderful!" Ruth patted her cheek again before turning back to the picnic tables. "Now, why don't you tell me more about yourself? Where are you from? What do you do?"

"I was born and raised in Philadelphia. I live down the block from Cheyenne in the brownstone I grew up in."

"With your parents?"

"No. They were killed in a car accident five years ago."

"I'm so sorry." Ruth reached out and laid a hand on Iva's.

"It's okay. I still think about them a lot, but the pain of losing them has receded a little with time." She took a deep breath and plunged ahead. "Anyway, I'm the co-owner of an event planning business in the city, Celebrate With Style."

"Do you do weddings?"

"Many. Our specialty."

"So, you know all the ins and outs to get someone married off?" Her pointed look at Cheyenne didn't go unnoticed by anyone.

"And, here we go," Daks said.

"Mom," Cheyenne groaned, though she was still smiling. She slung an arm around Iva's shoulders, leaning in close. "Don't worry, she'll probably have you planning our wedding by the end of the day."

Iva laughed, nudging her with an elbow. "Not if I have anything to say about it. Too soon."

"Give it time," Daks said. "She'll wear you down. She certainly did with Burke and me."

"And you see it worked out fine," Ruth pointed out.

Iva attempted to change the subject. "There are a lot of wedding planners in Philly and the surrounding area. We love doing weddings most of all, and we're known for it, but we do anniversary parties, graduations, showers, formal events, fundraisers...you name it."

Ruth wasn't swayed. She fixated on wedding planning and asked so many questions Daks gave up on the entire conversation and went to check up on her children.

Twenty minutes later, Ruth stood, collected the empty water bottles, and headed toward the front door. "I'm glad you two are getting on so well," she said, shooting them a smile over her shoulder. "Cheyenne doesn't bring her girlfriends around often, you know."

Cheyenne groaned, dropping her head back against the sofa. "Mom, come on. Iva's not my girlfriend."

"Yet," Ruth said, a teasing lilt to her voice. She gathered a few stray soda cans too and headed for the kitchen, calling over her shoulder, "She's perfect for you, honey. Pretty, funny, and gainfully employed. You should put a ring on it before someone else snatches her up!"

Cheyenne dragged a hand down her face. "I'm going to kill her," she mumbled, then shot Iva an apologetic look. "I'm so sorry about her. She can be...a lot."

Iva chuckled, patting Cheyenne's knee. "It's sweet that she cares so much about your happiness. Even if she is a bit overeager."

"Overeager is an understatement," Cheyenne said under her breath, then sighed. "You're too nice, you know that? Putting up with my crazy family..."

"I like your crazy family," Iva said. "Especially you."

Cheyenne blinked at her for a moment, eyes widening, before she huffed out a soft laugh and bumped Iva's shoulder with her own. "Smooth talker. No wonder my mom likes you so much."

"What can I say?" Iva shot her a playful grin. "I'm charming."

"And modest," Cheyenne said dryly, the corners of her lips quirking up into a smile.

"That too." Iva nudged closer on the small outdoor settee until their sides pressed together, a warm line of contact from knee to shoulder. "But I meant it, you know. I'm really starting to like you, Cheyenne Moore. Crazy family and all."

Cheyenne ducked her head, but not before Iva caught the pleased flush staining her cheeks. "Yeah, well..." She cleared her throat, glancing at Iva through her lashes with a shy smile. "The feeling's mutual."

A few of the girls present cajoled their aunt Cheyenne off the porch. She was immediately surrounded by the boys, too. She protested only halfheartedly as the kids dragged her toward the lake, intent on dunking their beloved aunt in retaliation for her "cheating."

Still limping, Iva trailed behind, amused by Cheyenne's futile attempts to escape.

"I never cheat!" Cheyenne shrieked, struggling against all the little hands clamped around her arms.

"Help me," Cheyenne implored Daks, but she was clearly enjoying her sister's plight.

"Not a chance."

Cheyenne glanced back at Iva.

"I think I'll pass, too." Iva grinned, as she hobbled along. "This looks far too entertaining."

With a dramatic sigh, Cheyenne went limp in defeat.

The kids whooped in triumph, and got help from a couple of teenagers to heave her slightly into the air and toss her into the lake.

She surfaced a moment later, sputtering and glaring at their jeering faces.

Daks laughed, patting Iva's shoulder. "Don't worry. She loves it really. And the kids adore her, so she'll forgive them. Eventually."

"I can see why." Iva smiled, watching Cheyenne chase the shrieking children into deeper water after they all jumped in too. "She's really great with them."

"She is." Daks gazed at her sister with obvious affection. "Cheyenne's always been wonderful with kids. It doesn't matter where she is in the world, she always calls each of mine on their birthdays. Spoils them rotten at Christmas. She's really good to them."

"That's really sweet." Iva's chest felt warm, and she wasn't sure if it was because of the sun or the surge of tenderness the conversation evoked. Perhaps both.

Daks studied Iva for a long moment, a small smile playing about her lips. "I'm glad she brought you today. You seem like a good match for her."

Heat rose in Iva's cheeks. "Oh, we're not—I mean, it's not like that. We only just met."

"Maybe not yet." Daks shrugged, unconcerned. "But I can tell there's something there. A spark. And Cheyenne deserves someone who makes her happy."

Iva ducked her head, unsure how to respond. Her heart raced with a mix of panic and pleasure at the idea. It was far too soon to be having this conversation, yet she couldn't deny the connection she felt with Cheyenne.

Perhaps Daks saw something Iva wasn't yet ready to admit.

"Just think about it," Daks said gently, patting Iva's knee before rising. "I'm going to go make sure my hooligans haven't drowned each other yet. You two enjoy the rest of your day."

Iva watched her go, lost in thought. What exactly was she getting herself into here? She had a feeling life was about to get far more complicated.

Cheyenne

On the way home, as Cheyenne drove, she and Iva talked about their day. They both agreed that it had been a memorable one, but Cheyenne apologized for throwing so much at Iva at one time, and she apologized for her father and his views.

"Don't worry about it at all," Iva said. "I love your mom. I had a great time, and I've met far worse than your father. What's obvious to me about him is that he loves you and he wants what he thinks is best for you. He seems to respect your right to make your own decisions about your career, but maybe not in your personal life."

"I'm not so sure about my career either," Cheyenne said. "He hates the places I sometimes have to go to get a story, especially with the investigative journalism assignments."

"I guess I can understand that, especially if you're in danger."

"I admit, sometimes things can be...suspect in the places I go, but it's more than that. Let's just say, I can be following street gangs in Ireland and that doesn't get his dander up nearly as much as when I'm covering a water crisis in Somalia."

"Prejudice, then?"

Cheyenne sighed. "Not that he'll come right out and say, but all the signs are there."

"How is he with Italians?"

Cheyenne glanced over at Iva. "Depends. Are you Catholic?"

Iva scoffed. "I'm gay. What do you think?"

"Raised Catholic, though?"

"Yes, and no. Mom went to mass for years while I was young and doing catechism classes. Dad mostly skipped it. Christmas, Easter, funerals, and weddings."

"Your mom stopped going?"

"When I came out to them in high school, yes."

"Was she afraid of what the church...the priests would say?"

"No. At least, I don't think so. I think she was becoming dis-illusioned with all the restrictions and such long before that. She was always a believer in loving everybody, no matter what, because the Bible says to love your neighbor as yourself. The diocese in Philadelphia...most of the larger church is, or was anti-everything LGBTQ and shunning gays and lesbians out of the church, plus they were always anti-birth control, anti-women in the priesthood, you name it. She had a hard time reconciling her personal beliefs with the practices of the church."

"Heavy topics," Iva continued. "Let's talk about something else."

"Like what?"

Iva smiled broadly as she recalled the day they'd spent. "I loved how playful you are with all your nieces and nephews."

"They're so much fun, and honestly, playing kickball with them is easy on me. You don't need a lot of space or a lot of gear."

"I was thinking of several things that happened involving kids today, but that's the big one, yes."

"By the way, how's your ankle feeling?"

Iva flexed her foot. "Not too bad. A little tender, maybe. I haven't actually played kickball since grade school gym class, and I'm not into going to the gym or anything, so I'm probably lucky to get away with just an ankle twist."

Cheyenne kept her hands on the wheel, but gave Iva a quick once over. "You don't do any sort of exercise?" *Because you look like you're in great shape.*

"I don't really need to. My job has me on my feet and on the run all the time. Two days in a row eating full meals is a lot for me."

"You don't eat at the events you put on?"

"Who has time?"

"I guess I never thought of it that way."

They grew quiet for a couple of minutes, then Cheyenne reached over and let her hand find Iva's where it rested on her knee, twining their fingers together. Iva didn't protest, which Cheyenne took as encouragement. "So," she said, emboldened, "does this mean I get to call you my girlfriend now?"

Iva ducked her head, but even though she was driving, Cheyenne didn't miss the grin she was trying to hide.

"If you want to, I guess." Iva shrugged, feigning nonchalance, but the pink in her cheeks gave her away. "Might as well make it official if we're going to keep spending time together."

"Is that your romantic way of asking me out?" Cheyenne teased.

Iva snorted. "You're never going to let me live this down, are you?"

"Not a chance," Cheyenne said, unable to keep from smiling. She gave Iva's hand a gentle squeeze. "But just so you know, I'd love to keep spending time with you. As your girlfriend."

"Yeah?" Iva glanced at her, eyes soft and hopeful, the flush in her cheeks deepening. "I'd like that too. It's a date, then."

"What is?"

"Big Italian family wedding in three weeks."

Cheyenne grinned, warmth flooding through her at the invitation. "Meeting the family already? We just started dating."

Iva chuckled, but she continued. "There's a wedding for my cousin on a Saturday across town. No kickball, but then you never know what's going to go on with him and his bride to be. They're nuts."

"Wait, will you be working during it? Is this a wedding you planned?"

"Oh heavens, no. Not in my family. Weddings are a family event, from engagement until the relieved couple leaves the clan behind for their honeymoon. They'd never use an event planner to do what forty people working and clashing together could do. Anyway," she took a deep breath and pushed it out, "Terri was supposed to be my plus one, and—"

"I'd love to go." She double parked in front of Iva's brownstone.

"Are you sure?"

"It's a date," Cheyenne said.

"Okay then."

"I've got a crazy, mixed-up couple of weeks ahead of me. I'm flying to Sao Paulo in the morning for a contract assignment so unless you could use some help to get inside with that ankle, I have to get home and pack my gear, but I'll get with you when I get back, for the dress code and the details, if that's okay?"

Iva flexed her foot again. "I'm good with the ankle and, as for the wedding, great."

"Now then, since we're dating, is a kiss to hold me over for a couple of weeks, okay?"

"You're asking this time?"

"Are you objecting?"

Iva leaned over and Cheyenne claimed her lips in a kiss. They lingered a little, but Cheyenne broke it off when the sound of another vehicle approaching broke through the romantic fog permeating her car. She watched Iva as she exited the car and made her way seemingly a little gingerly up the steps to her front door, then she sketched a wave to her and left after the driver of the car that had come up behind her, beeped at her.

Chapter 6 - Fakery, Fakety, Fake

♥

A Saturday Evening in Late-July

Iva

The Choudhury wedding reception was held in the glassed-in shelter house at a park and botanical garden with a view of the park's lake. The tables were covered with white cloths and adorned with centerpieces of colorful flowers from the gardens. The combination of soft indoor lighting treatments and the clear blue sky outside the opened out long side of the building gave them the perfect atmosphere for a romantic celebration.

As the all-American bride in traditional white and the groom in traditional East India wedding attire made their way to the dance floor, Iva and Jon watched them and their families. The bride's parents were beaming with joy as they watched their daughter and new son-in-law enjoying their first dance as husband and wife. The groom's mother was wiping away tears as she watched her son dancing with the woman of his dreams.

The families were clearly enjoying the celebration, but it was the interaction between the bride and groom that was truly magical to Iva. As the couple swayed to the music, they held each other close and looked into each other's eyes with what appeared to be love and adoration.

Jon saw it too. He nudged Iva with an elbow and whispered, "You'd never know they aren't really in love."

Iva shushed him under her breath, but loud enough for him to hear. Then she leaned in close and whispered back, "I think this is another one that will all work out in the end, so to speak."

"You think so?" Jon started to say, but stopped short and tilted his chin toward the main entry into the glass shelter house from the gardens. "Look who's here."

Iva looked across the room to see a very late to the party Terri, entering the shelter house. She swallowed hard at the sight of her ex. *What's she doing here?*

"Was she on the guest list?" Jon asked.

"No."

The man who had been with Terri the day she collected what remained of her belongings from Iva's townhome appeared behind her. "She must be his plus one," Iva said.

"Let me tell you something, honey. You've got it all over him."

"Except for one thing she couldn't get from me."

"Trust me, it ain't all it's cracked up to be, but then, you know that."

"Jon!" Her voice rose, and a few people turned to look at her.

"Did I say that?" he whispered back. His grin looked devious to Iva. He glanced back across the room. "Uh oh. Don't look now. Here she comes."

Iva looked. She couldn't help herself. Terri glided toward them in a gold sequined top more appropriate for a nightclub than a wedding that she paired with white slacks. She had makeup on that was a couple of shades too dark for her coloring, which she hadn't blended well into the sunburn evident on her neck.

Iva pasted on a smile as she watched her approach. She didn't want to make small talk with her, or say anything to her at all, but decorum and the job dictated that she be nice and unfailingly polite to all the newlywed's guests.

"Iva, Jon," Terri said when she was a couple of steps away. "Why am I not surprised?"

Jon gave her a look and in his best snark voice asked her, "Well, Terri, to what do we owe the pleasure of your presence here at a wedding you clearly weren't invited to?"

Terri rolled her eyes. "Oh, come on now, Jon. I'm friends with the bride's sister. She invited me as her plus one."

Jon raised a well-shaped eyebrow. "And your man friend?"

"He's my plus one."

"Rather presumptuous of you, but then you always did take and take without giving," Jon said.

Terri didn't seem swayed by his opinion of her. "That's why we waited to show until after dinner."

"But in plenty of time for the open bar," Jon shot back.

Iva could feel her fake smile straining. She didn't want to engage in any conversation with Terri, especially since she knew how much it would hurt the bride if she found out she had shown up uninvited. "Well, we wouldn't want to keep you from enjoying the festivities," Iva said, trying to wrap up the conversation.

Terri smirked. "Don't worry, I won't be staying long. Just wanted to make an appearance and see some old friends."

Jon spoke up again. "Well, I'm sure the bride and groom will be thrilled to know that their special day has become a reunion for you and your old pals."

Terri shot him a dirty look before turning on her heel and walking away.

Iva watched her go with relief.

"Well, that was awkward," Jon said.

"Understatement of the year," Iva replied. "Let's just hope she leaves soon and doesn't cause any other disruptions."

Jon nodded and they both turned their attention back to the seemingly happy couple, who were still dancing and smiling at each other as though they were the only two people in the world. Iva couldn't help but feel a twinge of envy as she watched them.

Iva didn't get her wish. Terri found her again twenty minutes later as she was observing the caterers wrapping up their clean-up in the kitchen.

"Hey, I was looking for you," Terri said.

Out of the sight of the newlyweds and their families, Iva felt no need to be prim and polite. "Whatever for?" Over Terri's shoulder, she saw Jon enter the kitchen and start toward them.

"I just wanted to let you in on something I heard, is all."

"Gossip?"

"No. My source is reputable."

"I'm really not interested."

"You will be if you don't get paid for this gig."

"Pardon?" Jon interrupted.

Terri turned to him. "You're like a bad penny. You just keep turning up."

He made a quick show of glancing around the kitchen, but Iva knew he followed Terri in there to protect her, not to check up on the caterers.

"Doing my job, is all," he said.

"Well, if what I heard is true, you better hope you get paid for this job. I hear this is a," she paused for effect as she made air quotes, "marriage of convenience. The groom out there married my friend's sister to get out of an arranged marriage to a woman back in India."

"Hmm, that just can't be," Iva said while she did her best to maintain eye contact with Terri and not look at Jon. "We've met with them several times. They're a lovely couple, and they're very much in love. And, he was raised here, not there. We've had nods to some of the East India customs, traditions, and dress leading up to the wedding, but he's very Americanized on the whole."

"Believe what you want. I'm just telling you what I've heard."

Jon stepped in. "Isn't your plus one out there waiting? He looked pretty bored the last time I saw him."

She gave Jon a dirty look. "Yeah, well, there's no alcohol, after all. Who knew? I promised him we'd go get a beer."

"Off with you then," Jon said.

She nodded at Iva. "Nice talking to you. Haven't missed you a bit, Jon." With that, she turned and walked away.

When she was sure Terri was out of earshot, Iva said to Jon, "Loose lips. Someone is going to get hurt in this one if more people like her know that."

"You know it. Sad!"

Chapter 7 - Family Wedding

♥

Iva and Cheyenne stepped into the grand ballroom, their hands entwined as they took in the scene before them. The room buzzed with laughter and conversation, while twinkling white lights, strung along lattice hung from the ceiling cast a warm glow across the guests. In the center of it all stood Iva's grandmother, Lena Romano, resplendent in her gold-threaded shawl, her silver hair pulled back into an elegant chignon.

"Ah, there you are!" Lena exclaimed, waving them over with a flourish. "Come, cara mia. It's been much too long."

Iva moved quickly into the embrace of the Romano family matriarch, her rock after the deaths of her parents. As she kissed her Nona's cheek, she saw her Aunt Cathy, her father's older sister, sidle over to join them.

"Nona, this is Cheyenne," she said, introducing her date.

"Cheyenne, this is my Nona Lena Romano and my aunt Cathy, my father's older sister." My spinster aunt, she wanted to say, but she held her tongue.

Lena reached out to Cheyenne and squeezed her hand in greeting.

Cathy Romano got between Lena and Cheyenne and extended a hand to Cheyenne. "You would think after years as an event planner, my niece would know how to properly introduce people. Cathy Romano; and you are?"

"Cheyenne Moore."

"You were holding hands with my niece when you came in. I would suggest you refrain from PDA's for the rest of the evening."

Lena Romano nudged her daughter. "You've room to talk of manners, mia figlia."

"You may not practice, but we're still a Catholic family," Cathy Romano went on to Iva, ignoring the controlled ire of her mother.

"Maybe we should go," Iva said to Cheyenne. "I don't want to be where I'm not wanted."

Lena interrupted. "Nonsense! You are wanted and no one is leaving." She looked at Cathy and waggled a finger at her. "It's not your child's wedding, and it's not your place to pass judgement."

Cathy had the good grace to walk away from her mother and drop the fight for another day.

"Sit, sit!" Lena commanded as she guided them toward their assigned table, past the buffet which several of Iva's aunts and cousins were stocking. It was already laden with platters of steaming Italian delicacies–lasagna, chicken piccata, risotto–all begging to be devoured. Iva's mouth watered at the sight and smell of it. Most of the couples she and Jon put together weddings for chose excellent caterers, but they always went for typical wedding dishes of chicken, fish, or beef for their main courses and only switched things up for their cocktail hour appetizers.

"You're awful quiet," Cheyenne said. "If you're upset, we can go."

"Far from it," Iva said as she gave her girlfriend an impish grin. "I was just thinking how much I miss a good, ethnic Italian, wedding reception."

An hour later, after the introduction of the wedding party and then a long line to fill their plates, they made it back to their table. A second cousin or third, Iva couldn't remember which, seated beside Cheyenne leaned in and squinted at her. "Aren't you that writer? The one who does biographies and ghostwriting for celebrities?"

"Guilty as charged," Cheyenne said, as she sliced neatly through a meatball on her plate.

"Wow! So, what's been your most memorable collaboration?" he asked, his eyes wide with curiosity.

Cheyenne glanced at Iva, who was watching her with equal interest. She smirked and started recounting an outrageous tale. "Well, there was this one time I was working with a famous actor–won't name names, of course–but let's just say he had an affinity for wearing nothing but his superhero costume while we conducted our interviews."

"Really?" Iva asked, her eyes lighting up with amusement.

"Absolutely," Cheyenne replied. "It certainly made for interesting work sessions."

"Sounds like it!" the man laughed, clearly impressed by Cheyenne's colorful career.

As they continued to eat and share stories, Cheyenne would glance her way, as if seeking permission to go on. Iva just let her talk.

"Alright, I'll share a different story," Cheyenne said, her eyes sparkling with mischief. "Picture this: I was in London for an interview with a big celebrity who needed a biographer."

"Ooh, do tell," a woman at their table said as she leaned in with curiosity.

"Okay, so there I was, waiting nervously in this swanky hotel lobby. It was the first time I got a potential biographer assignment. I wasn't even sure it was real. I was younger and knew I was pretty naïve. I had almost convinced myself I was being pranked when the man himself walked in—none other than Elton John!" she revealed, pausing for dramatic effect.

"Wait, what?" Iva's mouth dropped open; surprise etched on her face. "You worked with Elton John?"

"Oh, my goodness!" said one guest. "That's incredible!"

Cheyenne nodded. "It really was. It was one of the most memorable experiences of my career. I've been extremely lucky to have interviewed so many incredible people, but that one was definitely special. He's quite the character, you know. He interviewed me himself, and we hit it off immediately. We shared stories about our travels and love for music. Of course, he'd traveled a lot more than me, but he really seemed interested in my impressions of things. Before I knew it, I was not only his biographer but also his co-author," Cheyenne explained, a proud grin spreading across her face.

"Wow," Iva shook her head, her mind reeling from the revelation. Her gaze shifted to her plate, the uneaten cannoli suddenly losing its appeal. She couldn't help but wonder if their backgrounds were too different for a relationship to work. After all, Cheyenne had mingled with celebrities and traveled the world while Iva was just a simple girl who loved her cat, Cuddles.

"Hey, are you okay?" Cheyenne asked Iva softly, when their table-mates got up to go to the bar. She reached across the table to brush some stray strands of dark hair behind Iva's ear.

Iva forced a smile and nodded, though her thoughts continued to race. "Yeah, I'm fine. It's just...you've led such an interesting life, Cheyenne. I feel like I don't even compare."

"Hey, listen to me," Cheyenne said firmly, locking her brown eyes onto Iva's. "We're both here at this wedding, as a potential couple, because we're both looking for something real in our lives. My past experiences don't define who I am, and they certainly don't dictate the person I want by my side."

"Really?" Iva asked quietly, her insecurities still nagging at her.

"Really," Cheyenne confirmed, giving Iva's hand a gentle squeeze. "Now, let's enjoy the rest of this reception, okay?"

"Okay," Iva agreed, but as they resumed their conversation with the other guests remaining at the table, her thoughts remained clouded with doubt. She couldn't shake the feeling that maybe their worlds were just too different to ever truly mesh.

As the evening wore on, Iva increasingly struggled to keep up with the conversation. Between stories of Cheyenne's time spent with A-list celebrities and Cathy's pointed looks from disapproving eyes, it felt like a constant reminder of the chasm between their worlds.

"Hey, did I ever tell you about the time I interviewed George Clooney?" Cheyenne asked, clearly oblivious to Iva's discomfort.

"Seriously, Cheyenne? George Clooney?" Iva's thoughts raced, but she managed a strained smile and shook her head. "No, you haven't."

"Ah, well, maybe another time," Cheyenne said, noticing Iva's unease. "But hey, it looks like they're starting the chicken dance. Want to join?"

Iva hesitated, her doubts about their compatibility weighing heavily on her heart. But she knew she couldn't let this ruin their night together. "Sure," she finally agreed, forcing a smile. "Let's give it a shot."

As they made their way to the dance floor, Iva tried to focus on the silly dance moves and the laughter of the other guests. For a moment, she forgot her concerns as she clucked and flapped her arms in time with the music.

"See? This isn't so bad, is it?" Cheyenne teased, grinning as she linked elbows with Iva for the next part of the dance.

"No, it's not," Iva admitted, but her thoughts still lingered on their differences, gnawing at the edges of her happiness. As the song ended and the DJ transitioned to another upbeat tune, she turned to Cheyenne.

"Can we call it a night? The music and noise are giving me a headache," she lied, rubbing her temples for emphasis.

"Of course, let's get out of here," Cheyenne agreed, concern etched on her face. She wrapped an arm around Iva's waist and led her away from the dance floor, completely unaware of the storm brewing beneath Iva's forced smile.

"Alright, we're all set to go," Cheyenne announced as they collected their coats and belongings from the reception hall. With a warm smile, she held Iva's light wrap open for her, making sure it was draped comfortably over her shoulders.

"Thanks," Iva murmured, her gaze drifting towards the dance floor where couples were still swaying to a slow song. She could feel the weight of her doubts hanging heavy in the surrounding air, but she tried to shake off the feeling and focus on the joy of their friends' wedding.

"Did you at least have a good time tonight?" Cheyenne asked, her eyes filled with genuine concern as they made their way to the exit.

"Of course," Iva lied, forcing a reassuring smile. "I just couldn't handle any more noise."

"Next time, we'll bring earplugs," Cheyenne joked, wrapping an arm around Iva's shoulder as they stepped outside into the crisp evening air.

"Deal," Iva replied with a small laugh, trying her best to keep up the façade. But as they walked towards the car, her thoughts kept circling back to their differences, and she couldn't help but feel the distance between them growing wider with each step.

"Hey, did you ever hear about the time I got lost in Paris during Fashion Week?" Cheyenne asked, seemingly oblivious to Iva's internal struggle as she launched into another tale of her adventures.

"No, I haven't," Iva responded, giving her full attention to Cheyenne's story, hoping it would distract her from her own thoughts. As Cheyenne recounted her escapades, Iva laughed along, swept up in the excitement of the moment. She wanted desperately to believe that they could make this work, that they could bridge the gap between their worlds.

But as they reached Cheyenne's car—a compromise over taking Septa and possibly getting back so late they needed a cab anyway—and Cheyenne unlocked the doors, Iva couldn't suppress the nagging feeling that she was in over her head. She hesitated before getting into the car, looking back at the wedding reception with a mixture of longing and regret.

"Everything okay?" Cheyenne asked, sensing Iva's hesitation.

"Fine," Iva replied, forcing another smile as she slid into the passenger seat. "Just tired."

"Let's get you home," Cheyenne said, starting the car and pulling away from the venue. As they drove, Cheyenne continued to regale Iva with stories of her travels, completely unaware of the turmoil in Iva's heart.

With each mile that passed, Iva grew more uncertain about their future together. She wanted so badly to believe that this could work, but the doubts were like an anchor, dragging her further away from the happiness she had briefly tasted.

As the car pulled up in front of the row of brownstones, Cheyenne turned to Iva with a warm smile. "I hope you feel better soon," she whispered, brushing a strand of hair from Iva's face.

"Thanks," Iva whispered, her voice cracking under the weight of her emotions. She forced herself to return Cheyenne's smile, but as they stepped out of the car and walked toward their apartment, she couldn't shake the feeling that their once-promising relationship was now balancing precariously on the edge of a cliff, teetering between love and loss.

Chapter 8 - We Were just Getting Started

Monday afternoon
Iva

Iva sat at her desk in the Celebrate With Style back office, absently twirling a strand of her long, dark hair around her finger. Her heart thumped in her chest as she stared at the photo of Cheyenne Moore on her phone. She bit her lip, trying to suppress the butterflies that fluttered in her stomach.

"Okay, spill it," Jon demanded, leaning against Iva's desk. "What's going through that pretty head of yours?"

Iva jolted back to reality and sighed. "It's just...Cheyenne. I don't know if I'm ready for this."

"Ready for what?" Jon asked, raising a perfectly arched eyebrow. "Meeting someone new? It's been months since you broke up with Terri, and you're still moping around like Cuddles when he runs out of catnip."

"Nice analogy," Iva said, rolling her eyes. "But seriously, Jon, I'm not sure if I can do this again. What if I get hurt?"

"Sweetie, everyone gets hurt," Jon replied gently, patting her hand. "But that doesn't mean we stop living. Besides, you two haven't even had your first 'real' date yet." He made air quotes. "You're getting ahead of yourself."

"Maybe..." Iva hesitated before opening her laptop and typing Cheyenne's name into the search bar. As she scrolled through articles and social media profiles, she couldn't help but compare herself to the adventurous journalist.

"Wow, she's been everywhere," Iva murmured, her eyes scanning an article about Cheyenne's latest investigative report in some remote corner of the world. "She's so...bold."

"Bold looks good on you," Jon quipped, glancing at the screen. "Trust me, I've seen your wardrobe."

"Ha-ha," Iva retorted, but her thoughts were consumed by Cheyenne's accomplishments. How could she, an event planner who specialized in weddings and birthday parties, ever hope to keep up with someone like Cheyenne?

"Stop it," Jon said firmly, catching Iva's attention. "You're doing that thing where you doubt yourself. You are more than good enough for anyone, including Cheyenne Moore."

"Thanks, Jon," Iva whispered, touched by his support. "I just...I need to be sure."

"Take your time," Jon advised, squeezing her shoulder. "But remember, sometimes the best things in life happen when we take a chance."

Iva shook her head, then let her eyes linger on a photo of Cheyenne with a dazzling smile and wind-tousled sandy brown hair. "I just don't know if Cheyenne and I could ever work out," she admitted, her fingers nervously tapping at the edge of her desk. "I mean, look at our lifestyles. She's constantly traveling for her reporting assignments, while I'm here planning events."

"True," Jon conceded, leaning back in his chair, "but opposites attract, right? Besides, you might enjoy the excitement that comes with dating a globe-trotter."

"Or it could drive me insane," Iva countered, her brows furrowing as she recalled Terri's constant need for control. "Cheyenne seems like she's always on the go, and I'm not sure if I can handle being left behind all the time."

"Okay, valid point," Jon said, nodding thoughtfully. "But have you considered that maybe she's looking for someone who can ground her? You know, give her a sense of stability when she's away from home?"

"Maybe." Iva's voice was barely audible as she toyed with a paperclip, her thoughts drifting back to her breakup with Terri. It had left her feeling vulnerable and uncertain, and the thought of opening herself up to another person—even someone as intriguing as Cheyenne—was terrifying.

"Look, Iva," Jon began, his tone gentle yet insistent, "you can't let your past experiences dictate your future. Yes, things ended badly with Terri, but that doesn't mean it'll be the same with Cheyenne. People are different, and so are relationships."

Iva sighed, knowing Jon was right, but the fear still gnawed at her. "I just...I don't want to get hurt again," she whispered, her eyes glistening with unshed tears.

"Nobody wants that, sweetie," Jon empathized, reaching across the desk to give her hand a reassuring squeeze. "But you can't let that fear hold you back from finding love and happiness."

"Is it wrong that I'm scared?" Iva asked, feeling the weight of her vulnerability pressing down on her.

"Of course not," Jon reassured her. "Fear is a normal part of life. It's how we deal with it that defines us. So, are you going to let your fear dictate your choices, or will you face it head-on and take control of your own happiness?"

Iva looked at her best friend, his unwavering support shining brightly in his eyes, and felt a flicker of determination stir within her. She knew she had to confront her fears if she ever wanted to move forward, but that didn't make the prospect any less daunting.

"Jon," Iva began, her voice laced with trepidation, "I'm just...not sure if I'm good enough for Cheyenne. I mean, she's worked with celebrities and jet-setting millionaires." She gestured aimlessly in the air, as if trying to physically grasp the elusive self-confidence that seemed to elude her.

Iva absently twisted a strand of her dark hair as she stared at the computer screen, lost in thought. Jon, ever the observant friend, could see that she was still struggling.

"Alright, babe," he said, leaning onto Iva's desk and crossing his arms. "Let's dig a little deeper. What is it that really scares you about getting involved with Cheyenne?"

"Um," Iva hesitated, her fingers tapping nervously against the edge of her keyboard. She knew she was talking them both in circles, but she jumped out there again. "I guess… I fear putting myself out there again after Terri. What if I get hurt?"

"Fair question," Jon replied gently, nodding, patient as he always had been with her, and with Nathan. Patience he seemed to extend to many a blubbering fool. "But remember, every relationship comes with risks. If we didn't take those risks, we'd never find love."

"True," Iva conceded, but her expression remained clouded by doubt.

Jon could tell that she was still holding back. "Come on, Iva, spill it," he urged. "If you can't be honest with me, who can you be honest with?"

"Okay, okay," she sighed, finally giving in to his persistence. "I think… I'm scared that if Cheyenne and I get together, eventually she'll discover that I'm just… ordinary."

"Ordinary?" Jon repeated, incredulous. He nearly knocked over a stack of papers on Iva's desk with a flourish of his hand, but caught them just in time. "You, my dear, are anything but ordinary."

"Thanks, Jon," Iva said, a small smile tugging at her lips. "But you know what I mean. She's been around the world, worked with all these amazing people, and I'm just… me."

"Exactly!" Jon exclaimed, his voice rising with passion. "You're you–unique, wonderful, loving, and so incredibly talented. And as your best friend and business partner, I can say without a doubt that you're not ordinary, Iva Romano. You're extraordinary."

Her eyes glistening with unshed tears, Iva reached for Jon's hand and squeezed it gratefully. "Thank you, Jon. I needed to hear that. But, as much as I want to find love again, I don't think I'm ready for something new just yet," she admitted, picking at the edge of her desk. "Especially not with someone as amazing as Cheyenne. I need to focus on healing from my breakup with Terri and taking care of myself first."

"Good for you, babe." Jon's eyes softened, his smile understanding. "You know what they say–you can't pour from an empty cup."

"Exactly," Iva affirmed, nodding her head. She watched as Jon fiddled with a pen, twirling it between his fingers. "And right now, my cup is bone dry."

"Then let's fill that cup back up!" Jon declared, slapping his hand on the table. He leaned in conspiratorially, a mischievous glint in his eye. "First step: spa day this weekend. We'll have to do it Sunday, but massages, facials, mani-pedis... the works!"

Iva laughed, feeling the tension in her shoulders easing at the thought. "You're on. But only if we find a place that offers cucumber water. It's not a spa day without cucumber water."

"Deal," Jon agreed, miming a handshake in the air. "Now, about Cheyenne..."

"Right." Iva took a deep breath, steeling herself. "I should tell her how I feel. Be honest with her about everything." She tapped her fingers nervously on the desk before looking up at Jon. "I owe her that much, don't you think?"

"Absolutely," Jon said, nodding firmly. "Honesty is always the best policy."

"Thank you, Jon," Iva murmured, feeling a rush of gratitude for her friend's unwavering support. "I don't know what I'd do without you."

"Probably sign up for that pottery class you've been talking about for years and never actually join," he quipped, winking at her.

"Hey!" Iva feigned offense, swatting him playfully on the arm. "I'll have you know, pottery is an ancient and noble art form!"

"Sure, babe, sure." Jon chuckled, holding up his hands in surrender. "Just don't forget to invite me to your exhibition at the Louvre."

"Deal," Iva agreed, rolling her eyes but smiling nonetheless.

Monday Evening
Iva

Iva stood in front of Cheyenne's door, her heart pounding like a jackhammer. Taking a deep breath, she knocked softly and fidgeted with the hem of her shirt. The door swung open to reveal Cheyenne, clad in a casual t-shirt and cargo shorts, her sandy brown hair tousled as if she'd just woken up from a nap.

"Hey, Iva!" Cheyenne greeted her warmly, eyes crinkling with genuine happiness. "What brings you here?"

Iva murmured, "Hi, Cheyenne," and fought the urge to blurt out everything that had been weighing on her mind. "Can we talk for a minute? It's kind of important."

"Of course." Cheyenne stepped back, inviting her inside. "Make yourself comfortable."

Iva perched nervously on the edge of Cheyenne's couch, trying to gather her thoughts. She glanced at Cheyenne, who sat across from her, looking both curious and concerned.

"I wanted to talk to you about...us," she began hesitantly. "You're an amazing person, and I'm so grateful for the time we've spent getting to know each other."

"Thanks, Iva. I feel the same way about you," Cheyenne replied, her gaze warm and encouraging.

"Here's the thing..." Iva took a shaky breath, bracing herself. "I've realized that I'm not ready for a relationship right now."

Cheyenne's face fell slightly, but she nodded, waiting for Iva to continue.

"See, my breakup with Terri really messed me up. And as much as I wish I could just move on and start something new with someone as incredible as you, I need to focus on healing and taking care of myself first."

"Hey, I understand," Cheyenne said gently. "But you know, Iva, we don't have to rush into anything. We can just hang out, get to know each other better."

"Believe me, that's tempting," Iva confessed, her voice wavering. "But I think I need some space right now. It's not fair to either of us if I can't give you my all."

"Okay," Cheyenne agreed, a sad smile playing on her lips. "I appreciate your honesty, Iva. And I really hope that we can be friends, at least."

"Me too, Cheyenne," Iva responded earnestly, feeling a sense of relief wash over her. "You're an incredible person, and I admire you so much. I hope one day I'll be in a place where I can fully appreciate everything you have to offer."

"Take care of yourself, Iva," Cheyenne said, reaching out to squeeze her hand briefly before letting go.

"Thanks, Cheyenne. You too." With that, Iva stood up and headed for the door, taking one last lingering look at the woman she could have loved but wasn't quite ready for. As she stepped outside, she felt tears prickling at the corners of her eyes, but she held them back. She had made the right decision–for herself, and for Cheyenne.

Chapter 9 - I Propose...

♥

Cheyenne

Cheyenne wiped her sweaty palms on her jeans and took a deep breath before pushing open the door of Celebrate With Style. Her heart did a double take at the sight of Jon emerging from a back room, his eyes lighting up in recognition.

Crap. Of all the people to run into, it had to be him.

"Cheyenne Moore, as I live and breathe!" Jon exclaimed, throwing his arms wide. "To what do we owe the pleasure?"

His flamboyant greeting drew the attention of the woman behind the counter—Iva Romano herself. Cheyenne swallowed hard at the sight of her ex, taking in the dark waves of hair, the smoky eyes, the curves showcased to perfection in a clingy dress.

Get a grip, she told herself fiercely. You're here on business.

"Jon," she said with a jerky nod. "Iva."

Iva's eyebrows rose. "Well, well. Look who's gracing us with her presence." Her tone was dry as the Sahara. "Here to sweep me off my feet again, Cheyenne?"

Heat flooded Cheyenne's cheeks. "Hardly. I'm here on business."

"Is that so?" Iva drawled. She leaned against the counter, arms folded, skepticism etched into every line of her body.

Cheyenne's mouth went dry. Why had she thought this was a good idea again?

"I, uh—" She faltered, cursing her suddenly knotted tongue. "I need to plan a wedding."

"Oh?" Jon's eyes lit with interest. "For whom, pray tell?"

Cheyenne took a deep breath. "Me," she said. "I'm getting married."

There. She'd said it. Now to duck anything Iva threw at her and then convince her to play along... She hadn't planned for that.

Iva stared at her, dark eyes unreadable. "You're getting married," she repeated flatly.

Cheyenne nodded. Her heart thudded against her ribs, a caged bird desperate for escape. "Yes. That's—that's why I'm here."

"Is it now?" Iva glanced at Jon, who was watching the exchange with barely concealed glee. "And you expect me to plan this wedding of yours?"

"Well, I didn't..." She started over. "I was hoping you might, yes."

Iva's lips twisted. "Really? We broke up less than two weeks ago. You've replaced me already and you want to marry her now?"

"Um, not exactly." Cheyenne looked at Jon. She didn't want to make her proposal in front of him.

"Can we talk privately?" Cheyenne asked, her gaze flicking between Iva and Jon. "There's a coffee shop just a block away."

Iva hesitated, eyeing Cheyenne warily. "I don't know if that's such a good idea."

"Please," Cheyenne implored, desperation lacing her voice. "It's important. Think about it, okay? I'll wait there for you."

"Go, Iva," Jon commanded as soon as the door closed behind Cheyenne. "Sounds like it could be juicy." He leaned closer to Iva and stage-whispered, "Besides, you know you're dying to hear what she has to say."

"Fine," Iva sighed, relenting. "But you're not coming, Jon."

"Aw, come on!" Jon pouted. "I promise I'll be quiet as a mouse. You won't even know I'm there."

"Nice try," Iva said, rolling her eyes. "But no. She obviously doesn't want to talk about whatever is going on in front of you."

With a sigh of acceptance, Jon waved Iva off. "Alright, alright. Go have your little tête-à-tête. But I expect details later!"

"Deal," Iva muttered, before following Cheyenne out the door.

Iva

Cheyenne was sitting at a table near the front windows when Iva arrived at the coffee shop ten minutes later. She stared into a tall cup of something pink and frothy, her expression unreadable. Iva ordered herself a black coffee and joined Cheyenne at the small table, saying nothing. The ball was in Cheyenne's court now.

"Thanks for coming," Cheyenne said quietly, her fingers tapping nervously against the side of the cup.

"Start talking," Iva replied, taking a sip of her coffee. She was curious, but her patience was wearing thin. Whatever Cheyenne had to say, she'd better make it quick.

"Okay," Cheyenne began, taking a deep breath. "I'm just going to cut to the chase." Cheyenne's voice was steady now, her gaze fixed on Iva. "I'm proposing a fake engagement and wedding between us."

Iva nearly choked on her coffee, coughing as she set the cup down. "You're what?" She couldn't believe what she'd just heard. Was this some kind of joke?

"Look," Cheyenne continued, leaning in closer. "I know it sounds crazy but hear me out. This arrangement would benefit both of us."

"Benefit? How?" Iva asked skeptically, her dark eyes narrowing. The idea was absurd, but she had to admit, her curiosity was piqued.

"First," Cheyenne ticked off on her fingers, "we'd be able to avoid the pressure to find 'the one.' Second, our careers would benefit from the stability and predictability of a committed relationship. And third..." She hesitated for a second before continuing, "We already know each other, so there's no need for awkward getting-to-know-you conversations."

Iva couldn't help but snort at that last point. "So, you think because we dated for three seconds and broke up that we're perfect candidates for a fake marriage?"

"Exactly," Cheyenne said with a grin, seemingly undeterred by Iva's sarcasm. "Besides, it's not like we're strangers."

"Maybe not, but it's still insane," Iva muttered, rubbing her forehead in frustration. "This isn't 90 Day Fiancée, Cheyenne." Her mind raced with doubts, and she couldn't shake the feeling that this was a terrible idea. But part of her wondered if maybe, just maybe, it could work.

"Okay, let's say I entertain this ridiculous idea for a second." She thought to herself, I really shouldn't. Still, she plunged ahead. "What about the ethical implications?" Iva questioned, her voice heavy with concern. "A fake marriage goes beyond a white lie or a fib. We'd be lying to everyone we know and love."

"True," Cheyenne conceded, her grin fading slightly. "But think of it as an experiment. A chance to see if maybe we can make something real out of this. And if not, well... no harm, no foul."

Iva sighed, torn between her ethical qualms and the strange allure of Cheyenne's proposal. She bit her lip, her mind spinning with countless scenarios and what-ifs.

"Look, Iva," Cheyenne said softly, reaching across the table to touch her hand. "You don't have to decide right now. Just... think about it, okay?"

"Fine," Iva muttered, pulling her hand away and finishing her coffee. She couldn't believe she was even considering this ludicrous idea. But as she stared into the empty cup, she couldn't help but wonder if it might just be crazy enough to work.

"Maybe we should talk specifics," Cheyenne said, leaning forward with determination. "You're a business owner, right? I imagine the publicity from this wedding could do wonders for Celebrate With Style."

Iva frowned, considering the proposition. "That's true," she admitted, her voice hesitant. "But why are you so eager to help me? What's in it for you?"

Cheyenne shrugged, avoiding eye contact as she fiddled with the straw in her tall pink drink. "Look, my parents are always on my case about settling down. They don't understand the life of a freelance journalist. I'm sick of the barbed comments from my father. And, as much as the pushing from my mother annoys me, honestly, I'm kind of tired of being alone."

And I'm not going into a committed relationship with a woman I've had two dates with to fool her family on her whim. "Why me?" Iva pressed, her eyes narrowing suspiciously. "You barely know me. And from what little you've seen, I'm fresh out of a relationship and not exactly stable."

"True," Cheyenne conceded, finally meeting Iva's gaze. "But there's something about you that intrigues me. You're smart, independent, and you've got this whole 'I'm going to make it on my own terms' vibe going on. I think we could be good for each other–professionally and maybe even personally."

"Wow, you really have thought this through, haven't you?" Iva muttered more to herself than to Cheyenne. She sipped her coffee, mulling over the possibilities.

"I want to go all out," Cheyenne said. "The big wedding with the families, whoever will come. Everything."

Iva asked, "Do you have any idea what 'all out' entails? There's planning, coordination, budgeting, vendor management, logistics, design, guest experience—"

Cheyenne glossed over all of that. "I need to settle down. I need to be grounded somewhere." The look on her face was earnest as she finished with, "We could have a good thing."

Iva couldn't help herself. "To get to a potential 'good thing,' we first must have a wedding. You're saying you want it all." She brought up the costs again. "There are non-refundable deposits if things don't go according to plan, there are—"

Cheyenne waved a hand, feigning little concern. "Let me worry about all that. Let my father worry about that."

"Do you honestly think he's going to pay for your wedding to another woman? Your father? Thomas Moore?"

"He doesn't have a choice but to pay for at least some of it."

"His head might explode," Iva said.

"True that," Cheyenne continued, "and just imagine your ex's face when she finds out you're getting married before she does. She might explode too."

"Okay, you got me there." Iva couldn't help but laugh at the thought. "That would be priceless."

"See?" Cheyenne said, encouraged by Iva's laughter. "We'd be like a power couple. Two strong women taking on the world together. Plus, we both have busy careers, so it's not like we'd be smothering each other."

Iva nodded slowly, beginning to see the appeal. "You know, when you put it like that, it doesn't sound completely insane."

"Exactly!" Cheyenne exclaimed, her eyes sparkling with excitement. "So, what do you say? Are you in?"

Iva hesitated, a million thoughts racing through her mind. But as she weighed the pros and cons, one thing became increasingly clear–this crazy plan might actually work. And who knows? Maybe it would help her find the love and stability she'd been searching for all along.

"Give me some time to think about it," she said finally, standing up and reaching for her wallet. "I need to weigh all the options and make sure I'm not making a huge mistake."

"Of course," Cheyenne replied with a nod, a small smile on her lips. "Take all the time you need. But just remember, this could be the opportunity of a lifetime."

Iva nodded, feeling a mix of excitement and apprehension. She grabbed her purse and made her way to the door, turning back to look at Cheyenne one last time.

She almost went back and sat down again, but she steeled herself. "I'll be in touch," she said, before slipping out the door and into the bustling city streets. As she walked, Iva couldn't help but wonder if she was crazy for even considering this proposal. But she couldn't shake the feeling that maybe, just maybe, this could be the start of something amazing.

After a few minutes of walking, thinking, and fretting, she turned around and went back to the coffee shop. Cheyenne was still sitting at the table staring into her half-full cup of pink something or other. She looked up when Iva stopped in front of her.

"Alright," Iva said, extending her hand across the table. "Let's do it."

Cheyenne grinned, shaking Iva's hand firmly. "You won't regret this, I promise."

"Let's hope not," Iva chuckled nervously, as they sealed their unconventional deal.

"So, we're doing this," Iva began, her eyes narrowing as she considered the details. "How long are we talking trying here? A few months? A year?"

Cheyenne leaned back in her chair, tapping her finger on the table thoughtfully. "I was thinking at least three years."

"Three years?" Iva's eyebrows shot up, and she felt a tight knot forming in her stomach. "That's...quite a commitment for a sham marriage."

"Exactly," Cheyenne replied, holding Iva's gaze steadily. "It would give us time to actually get to know each other, build a solid foundation. Who knows? Our relationship might even develop into something real and lasting."

Iva rolled her eyes, but couldn't deny that there was a certain logic to Cheyenne's words. Still, she had reservations. Her recent breakup with Terri left her emotionally raw, and she wasn't sure if she could handle diving headfirst into another relationship–even a fake one.

"Look, I know it sounds crazy," Cheyenne said, leaning forward and resting her elbows on the table. "But think about it. We're both successful, independent women who understand the demands of our careers. We can support each other professionally and maybe even emotionally. And if things don't work out, we can walk away, no harm done."

Iva shifted in her seat, her fingers tracing the rim of her coffee cup as she sorted through her thoughts. She'd always been a risk-taker, so why did this feel so terrifying?

"Besides," Cheyenne added with a smirk, "think of all the fun we could have driving my ultra-conservative father insane. He's not exactly thrilled with the idea of me marrying a woman, let alone one as gorgeous and successful as you."

"Flattery will get you everywhere," Iva teased, but her laughter was tinged with uncertainty. She bit her lip, wondering if she could really go through with this charade.

"Look, Iva," Cheyenne said, a sudden earnestness in her voice. "I know you're scared. But sometimes, you need to take a leap of faith.

And who knows? Maybe we'll both end up happier than we ever imagined."

Iva stared deep into Cheyenne's brown eyes, searching for any hint of deception or insincerity. All she saw was a fierce determination and a vulnerability that mirrored her own. And in that moment, despite all the doubts swirling in her mind, Iva knew she couldn't let this opportunity slip away.

"Alright," she whispered, her voice firm with resolve. "I'm in. Let's get married."

"Really?" Cheyenne grinned, her face lighting up with excitement. "You won't regret this, I promise."

"Let's hope not," Iva replied, a nervous laugh escaping her lips. And as they shook hands once again, sealing their unconventional pact, she couldn't help but wonder if she'd just made the best decision of her life–or the worst.

Over the next few days, with Cheyenne on the road, on assignment, they found themselves constantly on the phone, exchanging emails, and taking part in video chats. They picked a date in November and began planning their sham wedding, and despite the unusual circumstances, both women couldn't help but get caught up in the excitement.

"Okay, so we've got the venue locked down," Iva said as she pulled up the spreadsheet on her laptop, her fingers tapping away at the keyboard. "Now we just need to complete the guest list, decide on a color scheme, and pick out our outfits."

"Right," Cheyenne agreed, her voice crackling through the speakerphone. "I was thinking maybe a deep purple for the bridesmaids' dresses. What do you think?"

"Sounds lovely," Iva replied, trying to sound enthusiastic. She paused for a moment, realizing that this whole charade was becoming more real with every decision they made. "But remember, it's just business," she muttered under her breath.

"What was that?" Cheyenne asked, not quite catching Iva's comment.

"Nothing, nothing," Iva said quickly, forcing a smile. "Just talking to myself. So purple it is. Now, about our outfits..."

"Definitely no pouffy princess dresses," Cheyenne declared, eliciting a laugh from Iva.

"Agreed. Maybe something sleek and elegant instead?"

"Perfect," Cheyenne said, "as long as mine isn't too femme. Oh, and Iva? Let's make sure there's an open bar. I have a feeling we're going to need it."

"Good point," Iva chuckled, jotting down the note. "Alright, I'll send over some dress options later today for us to review. Anything else we need to discuss right now?"

"Can't think of anything," Cheyenne replied. "Thanks for doing all this, by the way. I know it's weird, but I really appreciate it."

"Hey, it's just business," Iva said, trying to convince herself as much as Cheyenne. "No need to thank me."

"Right. Just business," Cheyenne echoed, a hint of a smile in her voice. "Well, I'll let you get back to work. Talk to you later?"

"Definitely," Iva confirmed, ending the call and staring at her laptop screen.

After hours, as she scrolled through the never-ending list of wedding tasks, Iva couldn't help but feel a strange mix of emotions. The anticipation of planning such an important event was thrilling, but the knowledge that it was all based on a lie left her feeling uneasy.

She thought about Jon. He'd begged for information after her meeting with Cheyenne, but she'd put him off, telling him only that Cheyenne was no better than the young man who'd walked into the business a month before looking for a quick fix to something. She hated lying to Jon most of all.

"Get it together, Iva," she whispered to herself, taking a deep breath. "It's just business. You can do this." She would tell him soon, once Cheyenne was back in town and they could work out a few more things, in person like when they would announce their engagement to Cheyenne's family and to Nana Lena. *And maybe we could have a couple of actual dates before we tell anyone, anything, so we can get to know each other a little better and arm ourselves with information.*

With those thoughts fixed firmly in her mind, she dove back into the planning process, determined to make this sham wedding as convincing as possible. After all, it was just business—or so she kept telling herself.

Lying awake in bed, Iva thought of Terri and the heartache she had suffered when she left. How long had it been since she'd last felt whole? Too long, she thought.

A vision of Cheyenne popped into her head. So beautiful in all her tomboy glory, so full of life. Iva wanted to help her, but she also knew that she couldn't let herself get too close. She had to keep her distance—until she could be sure; it was the only way she could protect herself.

Iva steeled herself against the temptation to dwell on 'what ifs' and took a deep breath. She could do this. She would help Cheyenne stand up for herself, but not get too involved with her. She would have some fun, placate Jon, and draw a line beneath it.

With a deep sense of trepidation and unease, she made her choice. She was going to help Cheyenne, but not fall for her. That was the only way this could work.

Chapter 10 - Free Falling

♥

Cheyenne

Iva and Cheyenne met at a restaurant, a small Italian place with romantic lighting and a view of the city skyline. They were both nervous, but as they sipped their drinks, their anxieties melted away.

"I'm so glad you suggested this place," Iva said. "I've never been here before."

Cheyenne smiled. "Shocking, you being Italian, and all."

"I don't get out much to do my own thing." Iva shrugged. "There's always a wedding or an event."

"Me either," Cheyenne said. "So, this is perfect for a first date."

"Except, it's technically our third."

"True."

The conversation flowed naturally as they talked about their interests and hobbies, and they soon realized that they had a lot in common. They laughed and joked, and it felt like they had known each other for years.

"Dessert?" Cheyenne asked. "Perhaps something chocolate?"

"How did you know?"

"I can't reveal my sources."

When their server stopped at the table mere moments later and offered a dessert menu, she waved him off. "Just bring us the chocolatiest chocolate thing you have and two utensils."

"Wait, I have to share?" Iva asked.

Cheyenne just gave her a big grin. "Just wait."

The server came back a couple of minutes later with a decadent looking chocolate lava cake, still warm and oozing with molten chocolate. Cheyenne wasted no time digging in with her spoon, savoring each rich and indulgent bite. Iva watched in awe as her friend closed her eyes in sheer pleasure, moaning softly with each taste.

"Here, try some," Cheyenne said, offering Iva a spoonful of cake and chocolate sauce.

Iva hesitated for a moment, but the scent of the chocolate was too intoxicating to resist. She tentatively took a bite, and her eyes widened as the explosive flavors danced on her tongue. It was unlike anything she had ever tasted before.

"Isn't it amazing?" Cheyenne said, grinning even wider as she watched Iva's reaction.

Iva nodded, still speechless. As they finished the last bites of the cake, Cheyenne leaned in closer to Iva, her eyes sparkling mischievously.

"Do you want to know my source?" she whispered.

Iva nodded eagerly.

"It's a secret," Cheyenne said, her lips curling into a devilish smile. "But I'll give you a hint. You're related to them. We talked at your cousin's wedding."

Iva pouted. "That could have been anyone there."

When their dessert was finished, Cheyenne suggested they do something they'd never done before. "How about indoor skydiving?"

Iva looked skeptical. "I've never done that."

"Neither have I," Cheyenne said, "but I've always wanted to try it."

"Me too!" Iva said, but then she patted her full stomach. "But maybe I should just watch you, this time."

Cheyenne shook her head, a playful glint in her eyes. "Nah, come on. It'll be fun! And it'll help digest that delicious cake we just had."

Iva sighed and gave in.

They arrived at the indoor skydiving facility and were quickly suited up in jumpsuits and helmets. Cheyenne was practically vibrating with excitement, while Iva couldn't help but feel a little nervous.

As they entered the wind tunnel, Cheyenne turned to Iva with a grin. "Ready?"

"As I'll ever be," Iva said, trying to keep her voice steady.

They stepped into the wind tunnel and were immediately blasted with a powerful gust of air. Iva clung to the wall, her heart was pounding in her chest as Cheyenne flew, her body twisting and turning gracefully in the air as she laughed and whooped with joy.

Iva watched in amazement; her nerves forgotten as she saw how much fun her friend was having. When Cheyenne motioned for her to join in, she took a deep breath and stepped forward, feeling the wind lift her off the ground.

For the next few minutes, they soared through the air, their bodies weightless and free as they laughed and screamed with delight. It was a rush unlike anything Iva had ever experienced before, and she grinned from ear to ear.

When their time was up and they were back on solid ground, Cheyenne turned to Iva with a huge grin.

"So, what did you think?" she asked.

"That was amazing," Iva said, still feeling a little breathless. "I can't believe how much fun that was."

Cheyenne grinned. "Told you it would be a blast."

As they made their way out of the facility and back to their cars, Iva felt a sudden surge of gratitude for her new friend. Cheyenne had pushed her out of her comfort zone, showing her a novel experience by getting her to do something she never would have done on her own.

"Did you actually plan that too?" Iva asked. "The skydiving?"

"I admit, I looked it up, but I wasn't lying when I said I'd never done it either. I wasn't sure if you'd be up for it," Cheyenne said with a shrug, "but I figured we should try something new and exciting together. Life's too short to always play it safe, you know?"

Iva nodded, feeling a wave of warmth wash through her. Cheyenne was right - life was too short to always be cautious and careful. Maybe it was time for her to take more risks, to try new things and see where they led her.

They drove back to the restaurant, where they said goodbye and promised to keep in touch. As Iva drove home, she felt a warmth in her heart that she hadn't felt in a long time. She was filled with anticipation and excitement for the future. She thought just maybe she and Cheyenne had found something special.

Now I have to plan a date... What to do? Where to go?

Chapter 11 - That Pottery Class

♥

Iva smiled at Cheyenne as they walked into Neighborhood Potters. The air was filled with the smell of clay and the buzz of conversations.

"This place is great," Cheyenne said.

"I'm so glad you agreed to come here."

Cheyenne nodded back at Iva and wandered around, taking in the various pieces of pottery on display.

"I just love the colors and patterns of these pieces," Cheyenne said as she examined a vase. "I'd love to try my hand at painting some of them."

Iva smiled and stepped closer to her. "Let's do it," she said. "What kind of pottery do you want to try?"

Cheyenne thought for a moment and then gestured to a platter with a swirled pattern around the edge. "That one," she said. "What color do you think would look the best?"

Iva laughed and shook her head. "I can't make that call for you," she said. "You get to be the artist, here. You pick the colors."

Cheyenne considered it for a moment before pointing to a few bottles of glaze.

"I think I'll go with blue and green," she said. "They look so nice together. What do you think?"

Iva smiled. "I think it's perfect," she said. "Maybe we consider them for wedding colors instead of the purple? Everyone is doing purple, these days."

Cheyenne smiled back. "Maybe." She grabbed a couple of paintbrushes. "Let's get started."

The two women spent the next hour engrossed in their painting. Cheyenne was surprisingly good at it, despite having no experience with pottery. Iva watched in awe as Cheyenne carefully applied the paint in intricate patterns, let it dry, then layered on the glaze.

"You have a genuine talent for this," Iva said.

Cheyenne laughed and dipped her brush in the glaze. "I guess it's just something that comes naturally," she said. "It's kind of like a puzzle. Put the pieces together in the right way to make it look good."

Iva smiled and nodded. "Well, you have an eye for it."

Cheyenne grinned and continued to work. As she painted, they talked and laughed, their banter rising and falling with the rise and fall of their brushes.

"I really like spending time with you," Cheyenne said. "This has been so much fun."

"I have to agree," Iva said. "I never thought I'd have so much fun painting pottery."

Cheyenne laughed and finished up her painting. She stepped back and admired her work. "What do you think?" she asked.

Iva looked at the piece and smiled. "It's perfect," she said. "It looks like a masterpiece."

Cheyenne beamed. "Thanks," she said.

The two women turned in their pieces to be fired, cleaned up and put away their supplies, then headed out of the cafe. As they walked, Iva couldn't help but feel a connection between them growing deeper. She felt like she had known Cheyenne her whole life, and the feeling made her smile.

"What are you looking forward to most on our next date?" Cheyenne asked her.

Iva spread her palms. "Well, I don't know," she said. "I guess that's up to you to decide."

Cheyenne laughed as she took one of Iva's hands and gave it a light squeeze. "I think I can come up with something."

"I'm sure you will."

Later that night, Iva and Jon both leaned back on his front stoop bench. She told him about her engagement charade, the upcoming wedding she'd been planning after hours, and the dates she and Cheyenne had gone on so far.

Although Jon seemed to force himself to remain composed, his shrinking posture told her he was taken aback by what he was hearing.

Iva didn't know where to begin, so she started with a summary of how the plan had transpired. She explained that what she felt like was a mismatch after her cousin's wedding, turned out to be cold feet. In fact, she enjoyed her company, and the time they had spent together.

Jon remained silent, and Iva took that as a cue to continue. She added, "Despite our seeming mutual attraction, our overly busy schedules of make it difficult to actually make time to see each other, but our sporadic dates have been a lot of fun."

Seeing Jon's lips move slightly, she knew he was ready to ask something, so she paused and waited for him to speak.

Jon slowly ran his finger along the wooden bench, unable to mask the disappointment in his voice. "Why didn't you tell me all this before?" he asked finally. "You should know I would support you and help all I could."

Iva looked her best friend in the eye and said simply, "I was scared. Scared of your reaction to it all and also afraid of what it could mean for the two of us and our business...good and bad."

Jon shook his head. "Focus on the relationship. Make sure it's right for you. The business - our business - is fine. We're doing great."

Jon's face softened even more as he looked into Iva's eyes. He said, "We've been friends for a long time, business partners for several years, and we've had a closer personal relationship...well, ever since your folks passed." He took a deep breath. "You're probably going to hate what I'm about to say, but I'm going to say it, anyway."

When Iva didn't respond, he went on. "I always felt like you being with Terri was a safety net to not be alone after your parents died. I never felt like she was right for you, and I think somewhere, deep down, you might have known that too. I just wanted you to be happy, and for a time, she seemed to make you happy."

"Now, I know I haven't been the most understanding lately," he said carefully, "but I want you to take this seriously. Make sure your feelings are real and that this situation works out for you."

He paused for a moment before continuing. "And again, don't worry about our business," Jon added with conviction. "It's going great and there's nothing to worry about. We don't need Cheyenne's help to be the best around."

Iva reached over and squeezed Jon's hand before standing up. "Thanks. I needed to hear that."

As she began walking back toward her house, Jon called out to her: "Go get 'em tiger!"

Chapter 12 - It's a Date

Time was not on their side. Between Iva's event planning business and Cheyenne's globe-trotting, freelance journalism career, their schedules were a logistical nightmare. They stole moments together when they could, coordinating lunches between meetings for Iva and assignments for Cheyenne and having late-night conversations that left them bleary-eyed but happy the next morning.

"Can you believe it's been two weeks since our last date?" Iva asked, running her fingers through Cuddles' fur as they video chatted one evening.

"Feels like forever," Cheyenne admitted, leaning back in a hotel room desk chair with a sigh. "But I've got some time at home coming up next week. How about we do something special? Maybe spend a whole day together?"

"An entire day?" Iva teased, feigning shock. "Are you sure you can handle that much time with me?"

"Guess we'll find out," Cheyenne shot back, a mischievous glint in her brown eyes.

As they talked, Iva's mind raced with possibilities for their upcoming day together. She wanted to show Cheyenne that she was serious about the growing feelings between them, even if their fake engagement had begun as a lighthearted joke. And while she knew they couldn't afford to let their secret slip, part of her longed for the world to know just how much this woman meant to her.

"Alright," Iva said, steeling herself for the leap she was about to take. "You plan your perfect date, and I'll plan mine. Then we'll compare and see who comes out on top, which one we do."

"Challenge accepted," Cheyenne replied, her voice brimming with confidence. "You're on, Romano."

Iva chose several activities in and around Philadelphia that involved food, but she didn't realize she'd done that until she and Cheyenne compared itineraries. Cheyenne showed her a list of things to do that didn't involve stopping to eat at all.

"I figured, we could eat as we went, whatever caught our fancy," Chey said.

Iva's mind whirled. "The activities we've chosen are all over downtown and a couple are out in the suburbs. I think we could arrange an all-day date that involves several of them without crisscrossing back and forth too much."

"Let's do it!" Chey said.

Iva gave her a sly smile. "But then, who wins the perfect date contest?"

"Ha, ha. In this scenario, we both do."

They started their day in the late morning at the La Colombe coffee shop on 19th Street, a favorite of Iva's, only a couple of blocks from her brownstone. As they waited in line, Cheyenne insisted on paying for their drinks despite Iva's protests. "What kind of fiancée would I be if I didn't treat my love on our special day out?" Cheyenne said. Iva finally relented with an, "Okay, but I get the next one!"

Iva ordered her usual vanilla latte while Cheyenne went for the Americano. As they waited for their drinks, they scoped out a cozy table by the window to sit at. But just as they went to grab it, another couple swooped in to claim it first.

"Rats!" Iva said. "Well, good thing we're faster than anyone on that surrey bike we're renting later!"

Cheyenne winked and led them to another table with a street view.

Once seated, Iva apologized to Cheyenne. "I'm sorry I had to go into the shop this morning. It's not a big event this weekend, but I had a few things I needed to make sure of."

"It's okay. Judging by our combined list, we've got quite a day and evening ahead of us."

They chatted happily about their plans for the day over their coffees. Iva was so animated telling a story that she knocked over her latte, spilling it across the table! "Whoops!" she yelped as Cheyenne quickly grabbed napkins to help clean up.

"Well, that's one way to make sure we don't sit here all morning," Cheyenne joked. A barista saw the spill and came over to help too, comping Iva a free replacement latte.

Next, Iva and Cheyenne headed to Neighborhood Potters for another pottery painting session. Iva had been surprised but pleased to see it on Chey's list.

They perused the shelves of ceramic pieces to decorate.

"Oooh how about these two mugs, so we can have a hers and hers set!" Iva suggested. Cheyenne nodded in agreement, and they got to work picking out colors and patterns.

When they couldn't agree on an overall pattern after several minutes, they decided the size and shape being the same would have to do. Cheyenne went bold with red and blue swirls on her mug while Iva painted some intricate flowers in contrasting colors on hers. They were focused on their work until Iva looked up to see Chey had a big blue smudge of paint on her nose.

Iva chuckled, "Looks like you got a little paint happy over there, babe!" Cheyenne crossed her eyes, trying to glimpse her painted nose, making Iva laugh harder.

When the mugs were finished, they wrote sweet notes to each other on the bottom before heading to the kiln. "These will be perfect for romantic weekend mornings together," Cheyenne smiled and squeezed Iva's hand.

For lunch, Iva and Cheyenne headed to the bustling Reading Terminal Market. The aromatic smells of spices, meats, and baked goods wafted through the air.

"Where should we even start?" Iva wondered aloud, feeling overwhelmed by the choices.

Cheyenne suggested, "How about we take a lap around to scope out all the options before deciding?"

They walked past busy stalls and eateries, everything looking delicious. Halfway through, like with the mugs, the couple realized they had completely different wants - Iva craved ramen but Cheyenne had a hankering for falafel.

"Looks like we're splitting up!" Iva said.

They agreed to get their own meals and find a table to share.

Iva waited in line for her shoyu ramen, foot tapping impatiently. Meanwhile, Cheyenne was overwhelmed deciding on falafel toppings. "Pickles or no pickles...hummus or tzatziki..." she debated.

Finally, they reunited, Iva slurping noodles while Cheyenne assembled her stuffed pita.

"Here, try some of this," Iva insisted, holding out broth-soaked ramen.

Cheyenne hesitated.

"Oh, come on, you've eaten raw bugs, halfway 'round the world!" Iva prodded.

Cheyenne laughed and finally took a bite. "Mm. You were right. That's the perfect comfort food for today," she admitted.

Iva just grinned and said, "I told you so!"

After lunch, Iva and Cheyenne took the tram to the Philadelphia Museum of Art and briefly considered changing destinations on their list to visit it.

"It's so nice out, though," Cheyenne said.

Iva agreed. "Yes, late summer in Philly and no rain. Doesn't get much better than this."

They saved the museum for another time. The two of them walked further into Fairmount Park to a rental stand to rent a surrey bike to tour the park.

"I'll steer first!" Iva volunteered eagerly when she saw the bike.

"Are you sure?" Cheyenne asked skeptically.

"Babe, I've got this," Iva insisted.

They climbed onto the quirky bike built for two with a side-by-side seat and took off slowly along a park trail. Iva seemed to swerve a bit, trying to get the hang of steering while pedaling.

"Tree!" Cheyenne suddenly yelled as Iva narrowly missed crashing the lumbering bike into an oak.

"Whoops, my bad!" Iva called out.

After a slightly wobbly start, the pair finally got into a rhythm. The breeze felt refreshing as they pedaled alongside the river.

Cheyenne rested her head on Iva's shoulder with a content sigh. Right then, Iva hit a bump on the trail, jostling them. "Bumps ahead!" she warned belatedly.

"I noticed," Cheyenne chuckled, just holding Iva tighter.

Two hours later, the couple climbed into a cab outside the park, happy to let someone else do the driving.

For dinner, Iva and Cheyenne headed out of the city to take a couple's cooking class at Sur La Table, Iva had booked in advance.

They arrived ready to make a tasty meal together. At least, Iva did.

"I hope we don't have to make creme Brule or something too advanced," Cheyenne said nervously.

When the instructor announced they'd be making homemade ravioli, Cheyenne audibly gulped. "It's alright, I'll be right here to help you," Iva reassured, giving her a peck on the cheek.

"I just eat it, I don't make it," Cheyenne groused.

They were shown how to knead the dough and roll it out thin. Having grown up the way she had in an Italian American family, Iva was a natural, swiftly rolling her dough into a perfect rectangle.

Cheyenne's dough was misshapen and stuck to the counter. "Ugh, I'm making a mess over here!" she complained.

"Here, add a little more flour," Iva suggested, helping dust the counter. She showed Cheyenne how to lift and stretch the dough into shape. With Iva's guidance, Cheyenne finally had smoothly rolled dough too.

When they filled and sealed their ravioli, Iva crafted perfect pasta pillows. Cheyenne's had uneven edges, with filling spilling out. But after cooking them, the homemade ravioli still tasted amazing. "See, we make a great team in the kitchen," Iva assured Cheyenne, who was proud of her accomplishment.

Finally, Iva and Cheyenne headed back into the city to World Cafe Live for some evening entertainment. They ordered cocktails and found their seats in the music hall to watch the band.

As the indie folk group tuned their instruments, Iva whispered "I hope this band is good!" Chey, ever the music lover–unless she was on deadline - shushed her playfully and said "Trust me, I read they're up and coming!"

The band started playing upbeat melodies with powerful vocals and skilled instrumentation. Iva and Cheyenne were soon swaying and singing along. In a sweet moment, Cheyenne reached for Iva's hand, looking into her eyes as they danced together.

When the band went for a crowd surfing stunt, chaos ensued. Cheyenne got bumped aside, losing Iva's hand. "Where'd you go?" she yelled over the music, trying to spot her love in the excited crowd. Just then, a beaming Iva crowd surfed back to Cheyenne, who just laughed and pulled her into an embrace. It had been the perfect date day, full of fun.

The three weeks that followed were a whirlwind of stolen moments and carefully planned outings in between events for Iva and assignments for Cheyenne, each one leaving Iva more certain than ever that what they had was real. And as their feelings deepened, so too did the stakes, leaving them both grappling with the consequences of their unconventional arrangement.

But for now, all that mattered was the thrill of the chase - and their growing, undeniable connection.

Chapter 13 - Put a Ring on It

♥

A Tuesday in late August...

Cheyenne held the door open for Iva as she stepped out of her car onto the busy street.

Iva's eyes took in the bustling city around them. With a shop at the edge of downtown to save on rent, and the brownstone townhome she inherited after her parents' deaths only a few blocks walk away from the shop, she didn't need to visit center city much. There weren't many event venues among the office towers.

She paused for a moment to enjoy the architectural details of the older buildings, to watch the people, and to take in the smell of freshly baked pastries and roasting coffee beans wafting from the nearby cafes.

Cheyenne smiled down at Iva, admiring her enthusiasm, and then gestured to the jewelry store across the street. "Ready?" she asked, offering her arm, which Iva gratefully accepted.

"Yes!" Iva said, squeezing Cheyenne's arm tightly. "This is so...I don't know how to describe it." She was feeling both excited and nervous.

Cheyenne chuckled, "That's alright. You don't have to describe it. I can tell just by looking at you."

They stepped off the curb and began to cross the street when a voice called out from behind them.

"Hey, lovebirds, wait up!"

Iva turned to see Jon emerging from Cheyenne's back seat and breaking into a jog. "Jon! We'd almost forgotten you."

"No way! I wouldn't miss this for the world," he said, panting. "You guys are finally getting this engagement thing done right and I get to be here for it. I feel like I'm living in a romantic comedy."

Cheyenne and Iva laughed, then linked arms again and continued across the street. Jon followed, talking excitedly about how he loved being a witness to the love of two people about to make a commitment to each other.

They walked across the street, the sound of car horns and the hum of people's conversations filling the air.

When they reached the jewelry store, they stood outside for a moment, admiring the glittering display of rings.

"Well," Cheyenne said, "let's go in and pick one out."

Iva's heart raced as they entered the jewelry store. The polished counters and sparkling display cases caught her eye, and she couldn't help but let out a gasp.

Cheyenne smiled knowingly, leading her to the engagement rings. "Let's take a look, shall we?"

The trio were immediately greeted by a salesperson. "Welcome! How can I help you today?"

Cheyenne gestured at Iva and then to the rings. "We're looking for an engagement ring."

The woman's face lit up. "Oh, congratulations! That's wonderful. Now, let's see what we can find for you."

The salesperson brought out several rings for Iva to try.

As she reached out to touch a particularly stunning diamond, Cheyenne's hand covered hers, sending a jolt of electricity through her body.

"Don't be nervous," Cheyenne whispered, her voice silky smooth. "I'm here."

Iva took a deep breath, feeling a sense of calm wash over her. She found herself drawn to a simple yet elegant ring, and Cheyenne nodded approvingly.

"That's a good one," she said. "It'll look beautiful on your finger."

Iva couldn't help the smile that spread across her face as Cheyenne took the ring out of the case and slipped it onto her finger. The weight of the ring felt comforting and solid, like a promise of things to come.

Jon clapped his hands gleefully. "This is so beautiful! I am so happy for you both."

Cheyenne and Iva smiled at each other, both overwhelmed with emotion. Then, as if by some unspoken agreement, they all stepped out of the store and back on to the street.

As they left the store, Iva's mind was reeling.

Jon was still talking excitedly as they walked back to the car, though now his attention had shifted away from the engagement ring and onto the type of wedding dress Iva should wear. "I think you should go for something white and airy, with lots of layers and delicate lace..."

Iva came back to the present and laughed. "We'll see. I've already been looking at dresses, and in all honesty, I've never thought of myself in anything like that, or any other sort of traditional wedding dress."

"Oh, don't worry," Jon said. "We can find you the perfect dress. This is going to be the most beautiful wedding ever; just don't you go all Bridezilla on me."

"Not a chance." Iva glanced down at the ring on her hand. *This is real. This is really happening.*

A late August Sunday
Moore Family Gathering
Ruth Moore

The late summer sun beat down on the Moore family as they gathered for their annual end-of-season picnic at the lake house. Ruth Moore beamed as she watched her daughters mingle with nieces, nephews, and other relatives.

Ruth spotted Cheyenne weaving through the crowd between the rows of picnic tables, hand-in-hand with her girlfriend, Iva. They seemed to search for someone.

"There you are!" Cheyenne called out when she noticed her mother. "Can you gather everyone together? Iva and I have an announcement to make."

Ruth's eyes widened, but she complied, gathering the extended Moore clan to the picnic area. "Your niece has some news to share!" she told them all excitedly.

Once most of the crowd was seated and everyone had quieted down, Cheyenne cleared her throat. "Thank you all for being here. This summer has been very special for me, largely thanks to this wonderful woman." She smiled at Iva, who blushed.

"We know it hasn't been long, but sometimes when you find the right person, you just know. So..." Cheyenne got down on one knee, producing the ring they'd picked out together. "Iva Romano, will you marry me?"

A chorus of gasps went up from the crowd. Little girls clapped. Billy jumped up and let out a whoop.

Iva nodded, at a loss for words.

Ruth shrieked and pulled them both into a smothering hug. "My baby's getting married!" she exclaimed tearfully.

Cheyenne's sister Daks pushed through the throng to embrace her sibling. "I'm so happy for you!" She eyed the ring admiringly. "Nice job, sis."

"Congratulations!" everyone chorused, clamoring to get closer and offer their blessings to the newly engaged couple.

In all the commotion, no one but Ruth noticed Cheyenne's father, Thomas, slip away wordlessly toward the house. She sighed, knowing he disapproved.

Later, after the hubbub had died down, Ruth pulled Cheyenne and Iva aside. "I'm thrilled for you, honey, truly," she said to Cheyenne. "But your father..."

"I know," Cheyenne said. "It's too soon for him."

"He'll come around," Ruth encouraged, though she didn't sound convinced. She knew all too well, Thomas could be stubborn for a long time.

"All that matters is that we love each other," Cheyenne said firmly. "Dad will see that in time. And if not..." she trailed off with a shrug.

Ruth patted her daughter's hand. "It's your life. As long as Iva makes   you   happy,   you   have   my   full s   u   p   -port."

Cheyenne hugged her mother tightly. "Thanks Mom. That means everything."

Ruth hoped her husband would see reason, but she refused to let him tarnish this joyous occasion. She would stand by Cheyenne's choice to marry for love, no matter what.

"Now then," she said, "we didn't plan for this, so there's no champagne. I really wish you had said something, Cheyenne. We could have had a proper engagement party."

Ruth eyed Iva. "You would know, dear. Do people still have engagement parties, or am I being old-fashioned?"

Iva smiled. "If they do, I wouldn't know. I rarely get involved until a wedding date gets picked and reality sets in."

Cheyenne squeezed Iva's hand. "Can't wait to plan ours. Like mom said before, I've got a pro."

"What about your family, dear?" Ruth asked Iva.

Iva said, "My folks were killed in a car accident five years ago and I'm an only child. I'm close to my dad's mother, my Nona Lena. And, I've got a big Italian family. *Some of whom accept me as is, and some who don't.*

Monday, because Cheyenne had to leave town Tuesday morning, Iva took a long lunch with Jon's blessing, and she took Cheyenne to see her Nona Lena.

The two women were quiet on the short bus ride from Rittenhouse Square to Little Italy, where Iva's father had grown up.

Iva took a deep breath when they got off the bus and she and Cheyenne approached her grandmother's house. It was time to share their engagement news with Nonna Lena and the rest of the family. *Whoever is here. Please, not Aunt Cathy.*

Before they could even knock, the front door swung open. "There are my girls!" Lena exclaimed, ushering the two of them inside with a sweeping gesture.

In the living room, Iva's aunt Cathy sat ramrod straight on the floral sofa, lips pursed. Iva suppressed a sigh. Her aunt had never approved of her sexuality.

"What brings you both here today?" Lena asked, bustling about to fetch drinks and cookies.

Cheyenne squeezed Iva's hand supportively. "We have some news, Nona," Iva began. "Cheyenne and I are engaged!"

Lena gasped, nearly dropping the tray of snacks. Then she let out a joyous laugh. "How wonderful!" She pulled them both in for smothering hugs and kisses. "We must celebrate!"

Cathy made a small disapproving noise but said nothing. Lena shot her a warning look before turning back to the girls, eyes twinkling.

"Tell me everything! When is the wedding? I can cook all your favorites, mia cara," she said to Iva. "And we must invite the whole family, of course."

Guilt gnawed at Iva. She hated deceiving her Nona, who had always been so loving and supportive.

"Well, we haven't set a date yet," she hedged. "But we were thinking something small."

Cathy huffed loudly at this. Lena waved a hand dismissively. "Small, big, what does it matter? Love is love. Leave everything to me!"

The aunt finally spoke up. "Really, Mama, there's no need to make a fuss-"

Lena whirled on her daughter. "No need? Bah! My only grandchild is getting married! It calls for a celebration!"

She turned back to Iva and Cheyenne, eyes misty with emotion. "Just imagine the flowers, the music... We will throw you a wedding to remember!"

Iva opened her mouth but couldn't find the words. The steely look on Cathy's face deepened her shame.

Sensing Iva's distress, Cheyenne stepped in. "We appreciate your excitement, truly," she said gently. "This is all so new. Give us time to figure things out."

Lena bobbed her head. "Yes, yes, take all the time you need. But this joyous news cannot be contained!"

She pulled a startled Cathy to her feet. "Dance with me, figlia! My heart is bursting."

"Really, Mama," Cathy huffed, even as Lena twirled her around the room. But Iva could see her aunt's stern facade cracking.

Watching the impromptu dance party unfold, Iva felt the tension leave her shoulders. No matter what doubts plagued her, Nona Lena's joy was genuine. For now, that was enough. It had to be.

As they left Nonna's house, Iva couldn't shake off the uneasiness that had settled over her. She knew they had started this fake engagement as a way to navigate their complicated lives, but now, as their feelings for each other grew more intense, the line between reality and fiction blurred.

"Hey," Cheyenne said softly, taking Iva's hand as they walked to the car. "I know that wasn't easy, but we did it. Now we just need to focus on making this work."

Iva nodded, trying to push her doubts aside. "You're right. We just have to be careful not to let anyone catch on to the truth."

"Exactly." Cheyenne squeezed her hand reassuringly. "We can do this."

Later that evening, Cheyenne stopped at Iva's brownstone. She shifted from foot to foot in the doorway. "I'm leaving early. My flight is at 6:00 AM. I...I wanted to see if you needed anything from me and to say goodbye."

Iva invited her in.

"Just for a minute...I mean, I know you went back to work today, and you probably had to play catchup—"

"It's fine, really."

As Cheyenne took in her surroundings, Iva approached her, a gentle hand on her shoulder. "I'm going to miss you, Chey. I... I hope it's okay to call you that."

Cheyenne nodded as she turned to her. She was feeling a familiar ache in her chest. "I'm going to miss you too, Iva."

They were standing in Iva's living room, their faces just inches apart. Iva's eyes were locked on Cheyenne's and Cheyenne felt her heart skip a beat. She couldn't believe how beautiful Iva was. Iva's lips were slightly parted, and Cheyenne couldn't resist the urge to kiss her.

Slowly, Cheyenne leaned in, her lips just brushing against Iva's. The moment was electric, and Cheyenne felt her entire body come alive. As she deepened the kiss, her lips moved hungrily against Iva's. She felt Iva's response immediately as she pressed her body closer to hers. She felt her heart race with anticipation as Iva's hands gently caressed her cheeks.

The kiss was passionate. Cheyenne felt her entire body tremble as the kiss deepened. She felt like she was in a trance, the room spinning around them as they continued to explore each other's lips hungrily.

She moved her hands up and down Iva's back, exploring every inch of her body. She felt like she was finally home, and she never wanted to leave the moment.

Iva responded as Cheyenne raked her hands through her tresses, and she felt electricity course through her body.

The kiss seemed to last for eternity, and Cheyenne wanted to stay in it forever. Her lips were aching for more, but she was content to savor every moment. Every touch felt like a dream come true, and Cheyenne felt like she was on the brink of something beautiful.

Finally, their lips parted, and Iva looked into Cheyenne's eyes. Cheyenne could feel the love radiating from her, and she felt like she was on the brink of a miracle. She felt like she was flying, and nothing else mattered.

Iva smiled, and Cheyenne knew she felt the same way. Nothing else mattered at all but the two of them in that moment, locked in a passionate embrace.

Iva wrapped her arms around Cheyenne's neck, and Cheyenne felt like she was finally home.

They stayed in that embrace for what felt like hours until finally they both pulled back and smiled. Cheyenne experienced a near trance-like state. She never wanted the moment to end. But all things must end, and Cheyenne reluctantly pulled away.

Chapter 14 - Deep Conversations

A Monday Night in Early September

"So, where are you now?" Iva asked.

"A Hyatt in Moline, Illinois."

"What's in Moline?"

"No idea, but it's close to Rock Island Arsenal. The trade journal that's paying me is in the flood control products business. Rock Island sits entirely in the Mississippi River and employs 6,000 people."

"Not a glamorous assignment, by the sounds of it."

"They can't all be," Cheyenne said. "It pays the bills."

"Can I ask a question?"

Cheyenne thought Iva's tone sounded sheepish. "You can ask me anything."

"Do you...do you have to take assignments like that? I mean...is money an issue sometimes?"

"It's a valid question and something you should know. I'm comfortable, Iva, but I'm not wealthy. I only get book royalties for books where my name appears on the cover along with whatever celebrity I'm writing with...and I'm only getting a small percentage. My agent negotiates ghostwriting fees for me. They're onetime things and she gets a cut. I take the articles, the oddball assignments...really anything that doesn't sound too risky to keep up interest in me and money flowing."

"Do you prefer doing the books?"

Cheyenne leaned back against the pillows on the queen size bed in her room and gave that some thought. "Sometimes. Often."

"Have you ever thought about writing on your own? I mean, writing books?"

"Occasionally, yeah. I have. But who has the time? I've got this crazy job and now a very demanding girlfriend, you know."

"Oh," Iva said. "Someone I know?"

"Intimately."

"Intimately?"

"Well, maybe that was a poor choice of word."

"And you a journalist." Iva made a tut-tutting sound.

Cheyenne grinned to herself. *I love sparring with her.* "If I was going to write my own stuff, other than the articles and exposes, I'd write fiction...or try to, anyway. Romcoms or something. Something totally different from what I do every day. It's the old adage; you don't want to go home and do what you do at work. I mean, do you really want to be planning our wedding? Our children's birthday parties?"

Iva coughed and sputtered at the other end of the line.

"You okay?" Cheyenne asked.

"Children?"

"Yeah. Kids. A couple of them, at least. Why? You don't want kids?"

There was no hesitation. "It's not that I don't or that I do. I never gave it a moment's thought."

"I guess we should have talked about this before I asked you to marry me." *And I'm only half joking.*

"We can talk about it," Iva said.

"Would you bear our children?"

Iva sputtered around on her end again.

"A leap too far?"

"I just told you I'd never given it any thought. Now you want me to carry them?"

"Neither one of us is young, Iva, but I'm a couple of years older than you."

When Iva was quiet for a few long moments, Cheyenne said, "I'm sorry. I didn't mean to scare you."

"Be honest with me, Chey. Is this about wanting kids, or about being alone?"

Cheyenne shifted on the bed and ran a hand through her hair. "Both. It's both," she admitted. *Damn, she can get things out of me so easily.* "I really want kids. A couple, anyway. I really like kids."

"That part was already very clear. And, I hate to say it. While you would be a great mom, I think you'd try awfully hard to be their friend, too."

"You know me pretty well, Iva Romano!" She drew in a deep breath and went on. "I've always thought of myself as becoming a mother one day, but there was always someone else in the dreams...a vague someone else, but someone was with me sharing in raising them."

They were both quiet for several seconds.

"Did I scare you?" Cheyenne finally asked.

Iva didn't hesitate to answer. "No, you didn't scare me. You surprised me, and not in a bad way. It's a conversation we can definitely continue, but let's do it face to face."

"Deal." Cheyenne chuckled. "If that didn't scare you off, what will?"

"I don't know. You're not an axe murderer in secret, are you?"

"I'll never tell."

They both laughed, but then Iva's voice came over the phone, more sober. "What scares me is more and more of our business–mine and Jon's–is becoming weddings. We love that. But…Well, it seems like one in every five or six is fake now. I feel like we're in dangerous territory and I want us to stop doing those sorts of weddings entirely, but I don't see how we can."

"I just never feel like I can take that first step," Iva said, her voice soft. "I can't say no. My heart bleeds for some people we've assisted over the last few years. And now…now I'm doing it myself."

Cheyenne nodded to herself, finally understanding what she felt was the actual issue. "It's scary, I know. Think about your clients you've already worked with. It's the same for you–for us. It's hard to do something that might change everything. But you have to believe that it will be different this time."

Iva said, "I don't know if I can. I keep thinking about Terri, going through so much of this before…the 'I love you' things we said, thinking it was all forever, and it didn't turn out the way I wanted to."

Cheyenne sighed. "I wish I could hug you right now. Hold you. Reassure you it can be different this time. You have to believe things can be different if you let yourself take that first step. That's how change happens, after all."

Iva was non-committal. "I guess," she said. "It's hard to trust people, especially when I've been hurt before. It seems we both have our issues."

Cheyenne said, "But we also have each other now, and we can work through them together." She sat up, a sudden idea coming to her mind. "Hey, Iva, what if we write a book together?"

"A book? About what?"

"About us. Our struggles, our fears, our, dare I say it, love? We can call it 'Love in the Time of Doubt'."

Iva giggled. "A play on 'Love in the Time of Cholera'?"

"Exactly. We could tell our story, and maybe help others going through the same things. Plus, it could be our way of taking that first step towards something new."

"I'm not a writer, Chey."

"But I am. How would it differ from any other book I've co-written...except more fun? You have the stories. I do the writing."

"I couldn't out any of our fake wedding clients like that."

"Two things. One, we'll be very careful of that and, two, we can both use pen names."

Iva was silent for a moment, considering the idea. "I like it," she finally said. "Let's do it."

Cheyenne grinned. "Alright, then. We'll start writing as soon as possible. Who knows, maybe it'll be a bestseller and we'll be able to quit our jobs and write full time."

Iva laughed. "Dream big, Chey. But I like where your head's at."

And with that, the two women hung up.

Chapter 15 - An Ethical Dilemma

Iva

Iva sat on the edge of her bed after hanging up with Chey, staring at her reflection in the mirror as she contemplated her situation. She had always prided herself on her ethics, her sense of right and wrong guiding her every decision. But now, as she started to fall for Cheyenne, she couldn't ignore the fact that their relationship was far from conventional or legitimate. It was more like so many of the weddings she took part in arranging that she felt guilty about.

She knew too; they weren't ready to get married, that their love–her love, anyway–was still in its early stages and that rushing into marriage would be a mistake. But she couldn't help but feel the pull of her emotions, the desire to be with Cheyenne growing stronger with each passing day.

Iva knew it was only a matter of time before she and Chey would have to make a serious decision about their relationship. They both wanted the same thing–to find companionship and true, lasting love–but their views on how to get there differed. Iva increasingly saw marriage as something that should only take place after true love had been found, while Cheyenne was eager to take the leap and make things official.

I've got to stop the fake weddings. I need to do that. I probably should call timeout on our wedding, too. But, do I want to do that? Could I do it?

Wednesday Afternoon

Iva stepped into the floral-scented paradise of Petal Perfection, her eyes drawn to the vibrant colors and textures. Every bloom seemed to beckon her closer, promising a sweet escape from the stress that had followed her like a shadow for weeks. Normally she called in orders, or she sent the client around to the shop to choose their arrangement blooms in person, but she needed to choose the perfect flowers to complete the vision she had for the 50th anniversary party of a couple that had been close to her parents.

"Ah, Iva Romano," came a voice dripping with insincerity. "Fancy meeting you here."

Iva closed her eyes for a moment, cursing her poor luck. She turned to find Sonia Steele standing just a few paces away, immaculately dressed as always. Her dark hair was pulled back into a tight bun, revealing a face that seemed to be perpetually locked in a mix of disapproval and disappointment. The corners of her mouth curved into a smile that never quite reached her eyes–frosty blue orbs that felt more like daggers than windows to the soul. She looked the picture of the perfect suburban wife if the perfect suburban wife was a poor loser. A headstrong, height-challenged brunette in her mid-thirties, she looked like she had paid a lot of money to have her nose made smaller and her chin made pointier.

"Hello, Sonia," Iva said, forcing a polite tone. "Just picking out some flowers for an event. You know how it is."

"Of course," Sonia replied, her gaze sweeping over Iva's outfit with a barely concealed sneer. "After all, we're both in the business of making dreams come true. Some more successfully than others, I might add."

Iva clenched her teeth but refused to take the bait. "Well, if you'll excuse me, I have work to do."

"Wait. Before you go," Sonia continued, stepping closer and lowering her voice, "I've been hearing whispers about your little venture with Jon. Some rather... unsavory rumors, suggesting that 'Celebrate With Style' might not be entirely on the up-and-up."

"Is that so?" Iva said, trying to keep her voice steady.

"Indeed," Sonia purred, clearly enjoying herself. "Word on the street is that you two have been organizing sham weddings. How tragic it would be if such information were to spread, don't you think?"

"Rumors are just that–rumors," Iva retorted, her heart pounding in her chest. "Celebrate With Style has always maintained the highest standards."

Sonia tilted her head, a sinister glint in her eyes. "Well, dear, I hope that's true. For your sake. After all, it would be such a shame for a promising career like yours to go down in flames because of something so... scandalous."

"Is there a point to this?" Iva asked, her patience wearing thin.

"Only a friendly warning," Sonia said, stepping back and adjusting her designer scarf. "Mind your reputation, Iva. You never know when it might come back to bite you."

With that final barb, Sonia turned on her heel and sauntered out of the shop, leaving Iva standing amidst the vibrant flowers, her thoughts racing and her heart heavy with dread.

Iva stared at the door Sonia had just exited, her mind reeling with the truth in the accusations that had been thrown her way. Her hand trembled as she picked up a bouquet of roses, their velvety petals a stark contrast to the thorns that seemed to have taken root in her own heart.

"Is everything alright, ma'am?" the florist asked hesitantly, concern etched on her face.

"Fine," Iva responded automatically, forcing a smile onto her lips. "These roses are beautiful."

"Thank you," the florist replied, visibly relieved. "Do you need help with anything else?"

"Actually, yes," Iva said, her resolve hardening. "Could you please recommend some flowers for an impromptu engagement party? It's sort of for my fiancée and me."

"Of course!" The florist's enthusiasm was infectious, but Iva couldn't help but feel a pang of guilt twisting in her chest. She wondered if Cheyenne felt the same unease when they discussed their upcoming nuptials.

As the florist bustled around the shop, assembling a stunning arrangement of blooms, Iva's thoughts continued to drift toward her relationship with Cheyenne. Their connection had been undeniable from the moment they'd met, but now, with Sonia's words echoing in her ears, she questioned just how genuine their bond truly was.

"Does she really care about me?" Iva thought, her heart heavy. "Or is this all just for show, to appease her parents and fill her personal space with another warm body?"

"Here you go!" The florist presented Iva with a breathtaking display of flowers, their vibrant colors a visual symphony. "This should be perfect for your engagement party."

"Thank you," Iva murmured, her gaze lingering on the flowers as though they held the answers to her unspoken questions.

"Is there a problem?" the florist asked, picking up on Iva's hesitation.

"No, it's just..." Iva hesitated, unsure of how much to reveal. "I'm worried about my fiancée and me. We're in the public eye, and there are rumors going around that our engagement might not be genuine."

"Oh, I see," the florist said sympathetically. "Well, if it helps, I've seen a lot of couples come and go through these doors–and I can usually tell which ones are the real deal. And the way your eyes lit up when you talked about your fiancée... It sounds like you two really do care for each other."

"Thank you," Iva said, touched by the woman's reassurance.

"Trust your heart," the florist advised as she handed over the bouquet. "And congratulations on your engagement."

"Thanks," Iva replied, forcing another smile before leaving the shop, her thoughts still plagued with doubt and unease. As she walked back to her car, the fragrant scent of the flowers doing little to lift her spirits, she couldn't help but wonder what the future held for her and Cheyenne–and whether their love story would bloom or wither under the weight of Sonia's accusations.

###

Friday Night

Iva sat on the edge of her bed, absentmindedly stroking Cuddles who lay sleeping next to her, oblivious. She stared at the silver engagement ring glinting on her finger–a constant reminder of her fake engagement. She couldn't help but feel a pang in her heart as she longed for a genuine, lasting relationship.

"Ugh, I can't believe we agreed to this," she muttered under her breath, glancing at a framed picture Daks had taken at the August picnic of her and Cheyenne grinning at the camera, after they'd made their announcement.

"Talking to yourself again, babe?" Cheyenne's voice rang out from the doorway, causing Iva to jump. "You know that's a sign of insanity, right?"

"Ha-ha, very funny," Iva rolled her eyes, placing the picture back on the nightstand. "I didn't hear you come in. How was your flight?"

"It was fine. Now, what's going on in that head of yours?"

"Nothing. It's fine. Work. Jon is in the office getting ready for another big wedding bash tomorrow. Last-minute stuff."

"Shouldn't you be helping?"

Iva sighed. "Yes."

"But?"

She drew in a deep breath and let it out slow. "I...I couldn't concentrate. I told him I needed to step out for a few minutes. Get some air. Feed my cat."

She let Cuddles get down. "It's just... I keep thinking about what would happen if our families found out about our little charade. It could ruin us both."

"Hey." Cheyenne walked over and sat down next to Iva, wrapping an arm around her. "I know it's not ideal, but we're in this together, right? Besides, have I ever let you down before?"

"Not so far, but it's only been a month," Iva teased, forcing a smile.

"Touché." Cheyenne grinned, tapping Iva playfully on the nose. "But seriously, I'm worried too. Not just about our reputations, but also about your business with Jon. If this gets out, it could really hurt Celebrate with Style. And I'd never forgive myself if that happened."

"Jon and Nathan would be devastated," Iva sighed, resting her head on Cheyenne's shoulder. She thought about telling her about Sonia, but she pushed the thought away. She thought about her own doubts too, but said instead of voicing them, "We've come this far; we can't back out now. We'll just have to be extra careful and make sure no one catches on."

"Agreed," Cheyenne nodded, squeezing Iva's hand reassuringly. "We'll put on the performance of a lifetime, and once our families are satisfied, we can go back to being our fabulous selves."

"Deal," Iva smiled, feeling a little more at ease. "Now, I've got to help Jon with the preparations for that wedding tomorrow. Lord knows he could use an extra pair of hands."

"Or two," Cheyenne agreed, getting up from the bed and pulling Iva up with her. "Just remember, we're in this together. No matter what happens, we'll get through it."

"Thanks, Chey," Iva said, giving her fiancée a quick hug before they left Iva's bedroom, a place Cheyenne typically avoided when she was in Iva's brownstone. There were some boundaries they hadn't crossed, even though sometimes Iva could feel the heat. She wondered if Cheyenne sometimes felt it, too.

As they walked downstairs, Iva couldn't help but think again about Sonia Steele's recent snide comments. The woman was a thorn in her side, constantly trying to undermine her and Jon's business. And now, with the fake engagement, she felt like she was giving Sonia more ammunition to use against them if she even had an inkling things were not as they appeared.

"Earth to Iva," Cheyenne said, waving a hand in front of Iva's face. "You're awfully quiet. Are you still worried?"

"Ugh, it's just Sonia, one of our competitors," Iva confessed, her brow furrowing. They stopped and stood in the living room while Iva detailed the encounter for Cheyenne. "Every time she opens her mouth, I feel like I'm one step closer to being exposed."

"Hey," Cheyenne said, gripping Iva's shoulders and looking her directly in the eyes. "Sonia may be a snake, but won't let her ruin our plan. We'll outsmart her at every turn, alright?"

"Alright," Iva agreed, taking a deep breath. She appreciated Cheyenne's unwavering support, but she couldn't shake the feeling that continuing this charade was wrong. She wanted a genuine relationship, not one built on lies.

"Let's go kick some wedding planning butt," Cheyenne announced, a mischievous glint in her eyes. "And remember, we're a team. We got this."

"Right," Iva smiled half-heartedly, trying to convince herself that everything would be fine. But as they left her brownstone and headed to the shop, the pressure and anxiety continued to mount, making it harder for her to focus on anything else.

"Jon will know something is up if we keep acting like this," Cheyenne whispered, as they entered the shop. "We have to put on a brave face and pretend everything is fine."

"Fine, fine," Iva muttered, plastering a fake smile on her face. "Let's just get through this and hope for the best."

"Deal," Cheyenne agreed, squeezing Iva's hand one last time before they dove into the chaos of last-minute wedding preparations.

But despite her best efforts to keep up appearances, the weight of their secret threatened to crush Iva, making it increasingly difficult for her to focus on anything else. She imagined Sonia Steele lurking in the shadows, waiting for the perfect moment to strike.

Chapter 16 - Cheyenne Reflects

Later, after Jon had gone home and Iva was locking up, Cheyenne reflected on their earlier conversation, as she had a few times that evening. She knew they needed to talk.

She took a deep breath and plunged in. "Iva I've been thinking. I'm worried that our wedding might hurt your business."

Iva looked over her shoulder at her as she turned the key in the lock and tested the door handle. "Why?"

"If people find out somehow that our marriage is a business arrangement, they might mistrust you or even question the quality of your work. They might think that you're not as experienced or as reliable as they thought, and that could hurt your business."

Iva frowned. "I hadn't thought of it like that," she said. "But you're right. It is a possibility."

"I'm not saying we should cancel the wedding," Cheyenne said. "But I think we need to be careful. We need to make sure that no one at all finds out about our arrangement, least of all this Sonia character."

Iva nodded. "I agree," she said. "We'll have to be very discreet."

"And," she hesitated, "just in case, we need to be prepared for the possibility that word might get out. We need to have a plan for damage control."

Iva sighed. "This is sounding like a lot of work," she said.

"It is," Cheyenne said. "But it's worth it. Your business is important to you, and I don't want to do anything to jeopardize it."

As they walked back toward their homes, the two women talked for a while longer about how to handle the situation. They agreed to be very careful and to put a plan together to handle the fallout in case word got out. They also agreed that, if things started to fall apart, they would be honest with each other and work together to find a solution. Cheyenne just wasn't sure what such a plan would look like or how they would pull it off if they managed to put something together.

Saturday Morning

Cheyenne stood in front of the only mirror in her house, the one above the bathroom sink, looking at her reflection. She had never been one to care much about her appearance, but today she couldn't help but notice how tired she looked after being up all night, tossing and turning, trying to come to a decision.

She thought about her work as a freelance writer/investigative reporter. She loved traveling the globe and meeting new people, but it was also dangerous and she had been in some close calls, and she knew it was only a matter of time before something bad happened.

She thought about Iva. She was kind, funny, and smart. Everything that Cheyenne was looking for in a partner. But Cheyenne also knew that Iva didn't take risks like she did. Iva was content with her event planning business and never strayed too far from home. Cheyenne knew that if she continued down her current path, they would never have a chance at a genuine relationship.

Always impulsive, Cheyenne had gotten herself into some jams. But it was also her impulsiveness that had her connected to a woman she knew she was falling for.

Cheyenne splashed some cold water on her face and looked back at herself in the mirror. She took a deep breath and made a decision. She was going to give up her dangerous lifestyle and settle down with Iva. It was a big change, but Cheyenne knew it was the right one. But, how to convince Iva that she was serious?

Her thoughts shifted. The Sonia woman Iva had told her about was a serious concern. Just when the two of them were really connecting, along comes this person who had Iva not only doubting her decisions but fearing for her professional life.

They needed a plan; a good plan to combat Sonia, or failing that, to do damage control if Sonia got a hold of the truth about the marriages of convenience Iva sometimes arranged or their own unconventional arrangement. What could they do that wouldn't make things even worse?

Cheyenne knew they couldn't just sit around and hope for the best. They needed to take action and come up with a plan. She walked out of the bathroom and headed to the kitchen to make herself a cup of coffee. As she waited for the coffee to brew, she thought about all the different scenarios that could happen if Sonia found out about their arrangement or for sure about any of the others she'd only alluded to when she confronted Iva in the florist's shop.

Cheyenne knew Iva had a reputation to uphold, and any scandal could ruin her business. She also knew that Sonia wouldn't hesitate to use that against her.

She took a sip of her coffee and sat down at the kitchen table. She pulled out a notebook and started jotting down ideas. The first thing they needed to do was come up with a story to tell Sonia if she ever confronted them. They needed to be prepared and have their story straight.

Cheyenne also thought about hiring a private investigator to look into Sonia's background. Maybe they could find something incriminating that they could use against her if things got ugly.

She knew Iva would be hesitant to take such drastic measures, but Cheyenne was determined to protect their relationship and Iva's business at all costs.

As she continued to brainstorm, Cheyenne couldn't help but feel a sense of excitement. This was a new challenge, and she was ready to face it head-on. She knew that her decision to settle down with Iva was the right one, and she was willing to do whatever it took to make it work.

With a renewed sense of purpose, Cheyenne went back to her notebook, determined to come up with a plan that would keep them secure. She wrote a list of potential allies that they could reach out to for help. Cheyenne knew they needed to have a network of trustworthy people they could rely on in case things went south. She thought of a few former sources and colleagues who might lend a hand.

As she wrote their names, Cheyenne couldn't help but think more about Iva. She knew this situation was putting an added strain on their budding relationship, but she was willing to do whatever it took to make things work out. Cheyenne liked Iva a lot for sure, and she was pretty sure she was falling in love with her. She knew for them to have a genuine chance at happiness, this was just a hurdle they needed to overcome.

Cheyenne glanced at the clock and realized that she had been working on her notebook for hours. She stretched her arms and stood up, feeling more focused and determined than ever before. She knew they had a long road ahead of them, but she was ready to face it head-on.

As she put away her notebook, she made a mental note to talk to Iva about her plan. She knew they needed to agree if they were going to make this work. *How do I approach it with Iva?*

Chapter 17 - And So it Begins

♥

The sound of the first guests arriving echoed through the hall as Iva supervised the catering staff setting up the hors d'oeuver tables. She allowed herself a small smile, confident that this wedding would be another success.

That smile faded when she saw a familiar figure marching towards her, scowling. Sonia.

"What are you doing here?" Iva demanded.

"I should ask you the same thing," Sonia hissed, arms crossed. "Because this venue is booked under my client's name for today."

Iva's stomach dropped. "That's impossible. I have a signed contract for the Hayes-Parker wedding here."

"Well, it seems there's been a double booking," Sonia said. "My client booked this site over a month ago."

"Check again," Iva replied through gritted teeth, grabbing her paperwork. "My contract is dated several months back."

As the two wedding planners stood locked in a glare, Jon hurried over. "What's going on here?" he asked as he got between the two glaring women. "The wedding party will arrive in twenty minutes."

Iva quickly explained the situation. Jon's eyes narrowed at Sonia. "I assure you, we have the valid contract for this date."

Sonia scoffed. "I think I know how to run my business! Now get your stuff and clear out before I call security. I have an evening reception to get set up."

"You'll do no such thing," Jon said. "Iva, call the venue manager and sort this out. I'll deal with Ms. Saboteur here."

As Iva hurried away, Jon stepped closer to Sonia. "Did you really think you could just barge in here and disrupt this wedding? You must be out of your mind."

Sonia held her chin high. "When they realize you've illegally double-booked the venue, any rational couple will hire me to plan their wedding instead."

Jon laughed derisively. "Illegally? Really? I see what this is about. You're trying to slander Iva because you know she's more talented than you'll ever be."

Before Sonia could retort, Iva returned looking vindicated. "Just as I thought, the manager confirmed we have the only booking for today." She turned to Sonia. "You need to leave. Now."

Sonia glared daggers at them both, then snatched up her purse and stalked away. Iva and Jon exchanged relieved looks; the crisis averted.

"What a debacle!" Jon exclaimed. "Trying to ruin a wedding just to steal business."

Iva shook her head. "Unbelievable. But at least the wedding's still on."

"Of course. No thanks to that wretch," Jon replied. "Now come on, we've got a dream wedding to pull off!"

Reassured that Sonia's scheme had failed, Iva got back to work, more motivated than ever. She wouldn't let anything ruin this beautiful couple's big day.

Chapter 18 – No Help Wanted

❤

Monday Morning
Iva

The morning sun shone through the front shop windows casting a warm glow over the busy office of Celebrate With Style, where Iva and Jon were hard at work finalizing details for another upcoming wedding.

"No rest for the weary or the wicked," Jon singsonged.

Iva's fingers flew across her keyboard, but her mind was far from the task at hand. With each passing moment, the nagging voice in her head grew louder, screaming that Sonia Steele would soon discover their secret and ruin everything. She stopped working and started worrying.

"Hey, are you okay?" Jon asked, concern lacing his voice as he looked up from his laptop. "You've been staring at that same email for ten minutes."

Iva blinked rapidly, trying to refocus on her work. "Yeah, I'm fine," she lied, forcing a smile. "Just...distracted. It was a long weekend, wasn't it?"

"Forget about Sonia. She's nuts, after all."

Iva sighed.

"Is there something else? This is our busiest time of the year, every year, and you usually thrive on this stuff."

"Maybe I'm just coming down with something," Iva offered.

"Is it Cheyenne? Because if it is, I'll have to have a heart to heart with her," Jon reassured her, placing a comforting hand on her shoulder. "I'll get it all smoothed out."

"Thanks," Iva murmured, though she couldn't shake the feeling that this time, things might not work out so smoothly. "And since when are you and Cheyenne buddy, buddy?"

Jon flipped a hand at her. "You know me, babe. I can talk to anybody. Me and Chey, we're good."

As the day wore on, Iva's worries continued to mount, and she found it increasingly difficult to concentrate on anything other than Sonia's antics and ultimately on her fake engagement. Her usually impeccable attention to detail slipped, causing her to make uncharacteristic mistakes–like accidentally ordering peonies instead of roses for a bridal bouquet, or double-booking a venue for two different events.

"Seriously, Iva?" Jon questioned her later in the day with raised eyebrows. "What's really going on with you? This isn't like you at all."

"Nothing, I just..." Iva hesitated, swallowing nervously as she considered telling him the truth. But the potential fallout felt too risky, and she opted for evasion instead. "I guess I'm just a little stressed about everything." "Everything" felt like an understatement. The strain of keeping up appearances was taking its toll.

Jon didn't buy into her excuse. He stood and moved toward her desk. "Everything meaning what? Your wedding? You've had that planned, other than a date and an exact location. Cut me out of the entire process, too, I might add. No," he leaned against the edge of the desk and tapped a finger against his chin, "it's more than that."

Iva moaned to Jon, "I knew better than to agree to all of this with Cheyenne."

"She's not Terri." His tone was matter of fact.

"No. You're right, and I know that. But, this is crazy. I mean, I might have married her somewhere down the line, if this was all real, but—"

"So, you admit you love her?"

"That's a strong word."

"But, you do." It wasn't a question.

"Yes. At least, I'm falling...okay, falling hard, but it's very soon, and the feelings aren't mutual."

"Don't be so sure."

"I've never been more sure."

"Then you've never been more wrong. Is she in town?"

"Yes, why?"

"Is she working on an assignment right now?"

"I've no idea."

"Call her then and get her in here," Jon commanded.

Iva gave him a raised eyebrow look, but he made a scoffing hand motion toward her phone and moved back over to his own desk.

Cheyenne arrived ten minutes after Iva called, carrying a paper notebook.

Jon pulled his desk chair over to Iva's desk and directed, "Chey, sit."

She did as she was told.

"The reason I called this meeting...was because I always wanted to say that." When neither woman cracked a smile, he went on. "Iva, honey, you need to tell Chey how you feel."

Iva hated being put on the spot. She played dumb. "About what?"

"About how you feel about her."

"I...I..." She looked at Cheyenne's face. Chey's eyes were on her. She appeared interested in what was going on and maybe a little unsure. Iva vowed to get back at Jon, swallowed her pride, and said, "Chey, I'm scared. I'm falling in love with you, and I don't think...No, I know I'm not ready for that yet."

Cheyenne set the notebook she'd been clutching down and reached for Iva's hand. She gave it a light squeeze. "I know I've fallen in love with you. I love you, Iva."

She shushed Iva when she spoke. "Let me finish. I was going to say, but I know where you are and there is no rush. We can take as long as you need."

"Aww," Jon said. "That's sweet. Now then, I'll leave you two alone to discuss all the things you need to discuss. Just pretend I'm not here." He went into the front of the shop.

Iva whispered to Cheyenne, "He can hear everything." Jon faked a cough from somewhere in the front, punctuating her point.

She lowered her voice even further. "He called you here because he could see I was twisted up about something, but he doesn't know about Sonia."

Cheyenne whispered back, "Should we tell him?"

Iva shuddered. "There's more you don't know." She filled Cheyenne in quickly about the incident at the reception hall over the weekend. "Our little house of cards is wobbling, and I can't shake the fear that it could collapse at any moment."

Cheyenne opened the notebook. "Exactly! So maybe we should do something about it instead of just pretending everything's fine," she suggested, her brown eyes blazing with frustration. "I've got some ideas."

Still whispering, "Like what?" Iva asked defensively. "Come clean and risk losing our business? Our families? Our friends?"

"Maybe!" Cheyenne exclaimed, throwing her hands up in exasperation. "I don't know, Iva. All I know is that this isn't working, and something needs to change."

Jon poked his head through the door. "Anything I can do to help?"

As they stared each other down, the weight of their situation settled heavily between them. Despite their differing motivations and desires, one thing had become painfully clear: their fake engagement and the threats of outside exposure were tearing them apart from the inside out.

"Look," Iva said finally, her voice shaky with emotion. "I don't want to fight. We're in this together, right?"

"Right," Cheyenne agreed, her expression softening. "But we need to figure something out. This can't go on like this."

"Agreed," Iva nodded, feeling a tiny flicker of hope ignite within her. "Remember when we started all this?" she asked quietly, a wistful smile tugging at the corners of her lips.

"Are you talking about the block party or the proposal?" Cheyenne asked, chuckling softly.

"Both 'brilliant ideas' by you," Iva said as she made air quotes.

"Well, who knew then my brilliant little ideas would lead to so much trouble?"

"Little? I'd say everything's grown since then," Iva said, rubbing her forehead as memories of the past few months played like a movie reel in her mind.

"True," Cheyenne agreed, her own expression turning serious again. "But we can't change the past. All we can do is try to fix the present."

Iva nodded, knowing full well that Sonia Steele was the key to unraveling this tangled web they found themselves in. If they could neutralize Sonia's influence, maybe they'd stand a chance at salvaging their reputations and their relationship.

Just then, Iva's phone buzzed with a new message, momentarily breaking her train of thought. Glancing down, her heart skipped a beat as she read the sender's name: Sonia Steele.

"Speak of the devil," Iva muttered under her breath, her anxiety spiking as she opened the message. The contents only heightened her sense of unease: it was a photo of her and Cheyenne from their day out and about town, accompanied by a chilling message.

"Looks like your little lovebirds are finally coming home to roost. Better watch your backs..."

"Cheyenne, look at this," Iva whispered urgently, showing her the message. Cheyenne's face turned ashen as she read it, and they exchanged a worried glance.

"Things just got a lot more complicated," Cheyenne sighed, running a hand through her sandy brown hair. "We need to find a way to deal with Sonia—and fast."

As both women stared at the phone, their internal conflicts threatened to consume them: Iva struggled with her ethical concerns and the desire for genuine love, while Cheyenne wrestled with the fear of negative consequences and the impact on her family and Iva's livelihood. and livelihoods. They knew they had to act, but with so much at stake, the road ahead seemed more daunting than ever before.

"Let's talk to Jon and see if he has any ideas," Iva suggested, her voice shaking slightly. "He's been dealing with Sonia's antics for years; maybe he'll know what to do."

"What about Sonia?" Jon asked as he came fully through the door.

Iva quickly filled him in on her encounter with Sonia at the florist, then showed him the text.

Jon's eyes widened as he listened. When he read the text, his flamboyant demeanor giving way to genuine concern.

"Why didn't you tell me all this before?" He didn't wait for an answer. "It explains a lot. That stunt this weekend was just that, a stunt and not a mistake. Not that I ever thought it was anything but her being a giant pain in the patoot on purpose!" He paused and sucked in a big breath then stabbed a fist in the air. "Damn it, Sonia just won't give up, will she?" he muttered, rubbing his forehead. "Alright, let me think... there's got to be something we can do to put her off our scent and get her to leave you two alone."

Cheyenne offered her notebook with her ideas.

Jon paged through it. "I see lots of names."

"People who can vouch for me, for us."

"Sonia plays everything quick and dirty, Chey," he told her. "We have to fight fire with fire."

"Do you think she'll try blackmail?" Cheyenne asked him.

Iva answered. "I doubt it. She's more likely to go in for the kill. I'm surprised she hasn't already, especially after she was escorted out of that reception hall this weekend."

As Jon pondered their predicament, Iva and Cheyenne exchanged anxious glances.

"Wait a minute," Jon exclaimed suddenly, snapping them out of their silent reverie. "I might have an idea that could buy us some time."

"Anything, Jon," Cheyenne said urgently. "We're all ears."

"Alright, here's what I'm thinking..." Jon began, outlining a plan that was bold, risky, and just crazy enough that it might work.

As they listened, Iva and Cheyenne's expressions changed from worry to hope, and a renewed sense of determination took root within them.

"Let's do it," Iva declared, clenching her fists in anticipation of the challenge ahead. "It's time to face Sonia and put an end to her threats."

"Agreed," Cheyenne nodded, feeling a spark of excitement despite the danger they faced. "We can do this."

As the three of them worked out how to put their plan into action, a man in a Phillies ball cap crept out of the front of the shop, having overheard every word of their conversation. With a wicked grin, the eavesdropper pulled out his phone and dialed a familiar number.

"Hello, Thomas? You'll never believe what I just heard..."

An hour later, just as she was about to embark on her first part of Jon's master plan, a scheme so cunning it would have made Machiavelli blush, Cheyenne's phone rang. She glanced at the screen and groaned. "It's my mother."

"Uh oh," Iva said, her dark eyes wide with concern. "That can't be good."

"Put her on speaker," Jon suggested, his tone both giddy and apprehensive.

"Fine." Cheyenne pressed the button and Ruth Moore's voice filled the room. "Hey, Mom."

"Cheyenne! Your father and I have wonderful news!" Ruth bubbled with excitement. "We've hired Sonia Steel of Married with Magic to take over the planning of your wedding!"

Silence. The air in the room seemed to freeze as if someone had hit the pause button on reality. Cheyenne exchanged horrified glances with Iva and Jon. Of all the wedding planners in the world, her parents had chosen Sonia.

"Mom, are you serious?" Cheyenne finally choked out. "Why? I'm marrying a wedding planner, for heaven's sake!"

"Absolutely serious! We want this to be the perfect day for you and Iva, and we know Sonia is the best. She'll take care of everything so you two can just relax and enjoy yourselves."

"Relax?" Iva muttered, her knuckles turning white as she clenched her fists. "Far from it."

"Mom, you don't understand," Cheyenne began, her mind racing for a way to fix this without revealing their secret.

"Understand what, dear?" Ruth asked innocently. "Your father's finally coming around. It was his idea. Imagine it! Anyway, he and I just want to make sure you have the wedding of your dreams."

"Ruth..." Thomas Moore's deep voice rumbled in the background. "Let them talk. I'm sure they have a lot to discuss."

"Right," Cheyenne said, her voice tense. "We'll talk later, Mom. Love you."

"Love you too, sweetheart."

Cheyenne

As the call ended and reality resumed, Cheyenne stared at Iva, her heart pounding with panic. How would they handle this? If Sonia discovered their fake marriage plan, she'd surely expose them and ruin everything.

Iva's eyes were filled with fear, but also determination. "We can't let her take over our wedding," she said firmly. "She'll sabotage it somehow. We have to find a way out of this."

"Agreed," Jon chimed in, his flamboyant demeanor replaced by steely resolve. "But how do we do that without revealing the truth?"

Cheyenne chewed on her lower lip, her mind working overtime. She could handle her father's disapproval, but she couldn't bear the thought of letting Iva down. The pressure was unbearable, and she could feel the walls closing in.

"Maybe... maybe we should just come clean," she suggested tentatively, her voice barely above a whisper.

"Absolutely not!" Jon snapped. "We've come too far for that!"

"Then what?" Cheyenne asked, desperation creeping into her voice. "What do we do?"

"Let's think this through," Iva said, trying to remain calm. "There has to be a solution."

As they huddled together again, racking their brains for a way to salvage their plan, Cheyenne couldn't help but wonder if their entire charade was about to come crashing down around them. The thought sent shivers down her spine, but she knew one thing for certain: she wouldn't give up without a fight.

She stood. "Don't worry about Sonia from the planning end of this. I'll talk to my dad, smooth things out, take care of it. Let me handle it." She kissed Iva's cheek and marched out of the shop.

Cheyenne hadn't been gone ten minutes when Sonia Steele walked into the shop. Iva and Jon were both taken aback, but Jon recovered first.

"Well, if it isn't Sonia Steele. To what do we owe this displeasure? Didn't get enough comeuppance this weekend?"

"I'm here on business," Sonia said as she looked Iva up and down. She aimed her pointy chin at Jon and said in a nasal voice, "My business is with Iva. It seems I may have misjudged your assistant here."

"We're equal partners," Jon informed her, "and you're breathing good air in our business."

"Jon," Iva laid a hand on his arm. "Let her say her piece so we can all move on."

With an exaggerated sigh, Jon temporarily ceded to their rival.

"There," Sonia began. "I've been contracted by Ruth and Thomas Moore, of the Berwyn Moore's to plan your wedding, Iva, to their daughter Cheyenne."

Jon couldn't help himself. "You understand we plan weddings here, don't you? Why would you even try to make something like that up?"

Sonia waved a hand about. "I assure you my contract is quite real and it's simple, really. The Moore's don't think Iva should have to handle every detail of her own wedding."

"She wouldn't be," Jon said. "She has me, so she doesn't need you."

"Look, Iva, let me get right to the point. The Moore's are high society. Conservative high society. Their call took me by surprise. I know Thomas, and I know he would never condone this marriage."

"We don't need Thomas Moore's permission to marry, Sonia. We're adults."

"Tell me this; is this another one of your fake weddings? If it is, I won't be a party to that."

Iva bristled. "I assure you, it's not fake."

"You two are putting on sham weddings. Word gets around."

"That's slander," Jon said. "You have no idea what you're talking about."

"Oh, but I do. And, I would truly hate for word to get around to Thomas. I have my sources. And then there's the obvious. You and Cheyenne don't even live together. You haven't been seen out and about in society together—"

"Cheyenne doesn't subscribe to that life," Iva tells her. "Neither do I."

Sonia scoffed. "She travels the world. She writes about celebrities. She very much lives that life. The question is, why she chose you, or more likely, how you hooked her for this little scam. Fame and fortune for your little fly-by-night business here could be in it for you, but what's in it for her?"

Jon was incensed. "We've built this business from scratch. Our own sweat equity, so to speak. I abhor sweat, but that's beside the point. We're doing fine all on our own and don't need to trade on the Moore name, or anyone else's."

"Right. So, Iva, neither Cheyenne nor her father has ever put in a good word for you anywhere?"

It was Iva's turn to take issue with the insufferable woman. "We've already established that Mr. Moore doesn't approve. Why would we seek him out for recommendations?"

Sonia wasn't dissuaded. "Perhaps you're seeking more legitimate business."

"I've heard enough," Jon said. "You need to leave."

"Oh, I will, but consider this, you two. How about you get out of the wedding business entirely and stick to other events?"

Jon glared at her. "And why would we do that? Afraid of a little competition?"

"You do it, or I expose Iva to the Moore's and your sham business to the world."

"We don't have a sham business, so…" Iva shrugged. "Be my guest, I guess. Cheyenne was here a little while ago when you sent me your snide little text. We were working on redoing our wedding plans because Cheyenne and I had already slowed things down a little. We've only been dating a few months and we're moving fast, we've both decided. In the future, when we move forward, Jon will handle our wedding, not you. We're paying for it ourselves, not using Moore family money, thank you very much, and we want to do business with people we like."

Chapter 19 - Dealing with Dad

♥

The front door of the Moore family home in Berwyn creaked open as Cheyenne hesitantly stepped inside, her heart pounding in her chest. Her sister Daks, a beacon of support and understanding in the stormy sea of their conservative upbringing, greeted her with a warm hug.

"Hey, sis," Daks whispered, squeezing her tightly. "You ready for this?"

"About as ready as I'll ever be," Cheyenne mumbled, straightening her shoulders and bracing herself for what was to come.

The two sisters strode into the den, where their father Thomas sat in his favorite armchair, a stern expression on his face. Cheyenne couldn't help but notice how much he'd aged since she'd last seen him; the lines on his forehead seemed deeper, and his once-dark hair had turned almost entirely gray.

"Cheyenne," he said gruffly, barely glancing up from the newspaper he was reading. "What brings you here?"

"Dad, we need to talk about the wedding," Cheyenne began, her voice shaking slightly. "I appreciate that you and Mom want to help, but hiring Sonia Steele is just... it's not going to work."

Thomas raised an eyebrow, peering over the top of his paper. "And why not? She's one of the best in the business."

"Because..." Cheyenne hesitated, trying to find the right words. "Because this is our wedding, and we want to do things our way."

"Your way?" he scoffed. "You mean running around the world, never settling down, never giving your mother and me any peace of mind?"

"Come on Dad, that's enough," Daks interjected, placing a protective hand on Cheyenne's shoulder. "This isn't about her lifestyle–it's about her wedding to the woman she loves."

"Exactly," Cheyenne added, her voice growing more confident. "Iva and I want to plan our wedding together, with no interference."

"Interference?" Thomas snapped, slamming his newspaper down on the coffee table. "Is that what you call your mother's and my concern for your well-being?"

As the tension in the room escalated, Cheyenne felt a wave of panic wash over her. She couldn't understand why her father was so insistent on having Sonia Steele involved–unless he somehow knew the truth about their fake marriage.

"Cheyenne," Daks whispered urgently, pulling her sister aside. "Come on, let's get out of here."

Once they were safely outside their father's den, Daks turned to Cheyenne, her eyes filled with empathy. "Look, I know you're stressed about this whole wedding thing. Let me ask you something."

"Do you love Iva, Chey?"

Cheyenne didn't hesitate. "Yes."

"Truly want to spend the rest of your life with her?"

"Yes."

"I knew, but I wanted to hear you say it."

"I should be surprised, but I'm not. In all honesty, I was getting ahead of myself with the ring. I've only just figured out how...how much I feel for her, love her, in the last couple of days."

Chapter 20 - So Crazy it just Might Work!

❤

Cheyenne was speechless as her sister regaled her with the story of how she had figured out her true feelings for Iva.

"I see the way your eyes light up whenever Iva's near. The way your voice softens, Chey, when you speak to her. The way you lean in close to her whenever you're having a conversation. How your eyes linger just a bit too long on her curves and how you blush when she catches you staring."

Cheyenne tried to deny it, but Daks just smiled knowingly and hugged her sister.

"I'm so happy for you," Daks said. "Iva is a great catch, and you two make a cute couple."

Cheyenne blushed and shook her head, but deep down she knew Daks was right. She had been attracted to Iva from the moment she spotted her at the block party, and her feelings had only grown stronger with each passing day. She had thought her true emotions for the woman had remained a secret, until their engagement announcement, at least, but now here was Daks, spilling the beans.

"I knew too that Iva had strong feelings for you the moment I met her," Daks said. "I could see the way she looked at you, the way you looked at each other. Even my kids can see it. It's obvious."

Cheyenne looked around the living room of the family home, unsure of what to say. Daks's two youngest children were seated on the floor, wide-eyed with curiosity, watching the adults in front of them, quiet for the first time in as long as she could remember.

Daks went on. "Everybody can see it. You two were made for each other."

Cheyenne felt heat continuing to rise in her cheeks. She had never expected this conversation. "Maybe," she said, her voice trembling slightly.

Daks shook her head.

"Why don't you two just do it? Elope. Today. Leave this place, and never look back. You'll never find love as strong as this one."

Cheyenne's heart skipped a beat. The idea of running away with Iva held a romantic appeal, but she was sure it would be a total disaster. "That's a terrible idea," she said.

Daks smiled. "Maybe, but it's a wild idea. An adventure. It's something you'll never forget, and I know Iva won't either."

"We're both thinking we've been moving too fast. Now you want us to speed it up?" Cheyenne asked. "What if it doesn't work out?"

Daks shrugged. "Then you can blame it on me," she said. "But I don't think it will. I've seen the way she looks at you, too. I know she's as crazy about you as you are about her."

Cheyenne looked away, her mind spinning. The idea of running away with Iva was tempting, but she knew it would be a mistake. Still, the thought of spending days together somewhere, exploring and discovering, just the two of them... it was hard to ignore.

"Do it," Daks's kids said in unison.

Cheyenne glanced at the children. They were both smiling, their eyes bright with enthusiasm. She couldn't help but smile.

"Let's do it," she said, her voice barely a whisper.

Daks clapped her hands.

"Good!" she said. "Go home and start packing your things."

Cheyenne looked at her sister in disbelief. "Now?"

Daks nodded. "The sooner the better," she said. "Be ready to leave in the morning."

"Leave for where? I have deadlines. Iva has her business. Neither of us can just pick up and go, just like that." She snapped her fingers.

"You can. I've got an early wedding present for you two: open-ended plane tickets and the use of our condo in Hilton Head for a week. No parents, no Sonia Steele, just you and Iva starting your life together on your own terms."

"Daks, that's amazing, but...I don't know. Iva would probably never go for it."

"You don't know until you ask. If you want it, really want it, the two of you will make it work."

Cheyenne shook her head. She still wasn't sure if this was a good idea, but she couldn't deny the excitement she felt at the prospect of running away with Iva. Whatever the outcome, it was sure to be a wild moment.

Cheyenne stared at her sister, her heart swelling with gratitude. "Daks, you're...just wow. Thank you."

"Hey, that's what sisters are for," Daks replied, wrapping her arms around Cheyenne once more. "Now make your own happily ever after."

Chapter 21 - Stepping in It

♥

Cheyenne knocked on Iva's door, her heart racing. The brownstone loomed above her, elegant and intimidating like the woman she'd come to see.

When Iva answered, her dark eyes widened in surprise. "Chey? What's going on? Where did you go?" she asked, concern etched across her face.

"Can I come in?" Cheyenne replied, her voice barely a whisper. "We need to talk."

"Of course." Iva stepped aside, allowing Cheyenne into her home. Cuddles the cat greeted her with a purr, winding around her legs. Cheyenne couldn't help but smile at the affectionate feline.

She didn't pick up the cat as usual or even move from the entryway. "I went to see my dad," she began hesitantly. "I asked him to cancel the contract with Sonia."

"Did you tell him why?"

"I told him we wanted to plan our own wedding."

"How did he take it? I mean...do you think...think he knows?"

"I don't know what he knows. He was mad at the world when I walked in, so..." She spread her hands in a defeated motion. "Daks was there. She got me out of his range before I could really argue with him and stir him up even more."

Iva let out a heavy breath. Let's sit. I have something to tell you.

Cheyenne could only imagine what Iva was about to say as she followed her to the sofa. She wasn't quite prepared for what she said.

"After you left, Sonia came into the shop."

"Oh..."

"It was bad. Jon, bless him, did his best boxer impression, but she knows what we've been up to, and she's not afraid to tell your dad and everyone else in the world all about it. She had the nerve to try to use it as blackmail first to get Jon and I out of the wedding business in Philly entirely."

"Iva, I'm so sorry. This is all my fault."

Iva shook her head. "No. No, it isn't. We've been doing fake marriages for a few years now. We've kept it up, so this was bound to happen. It's our fault. Mine and Jon's."

Cheyenne's brain whirred. "So, Jon's big plan is out, but I have all those contacts I wrote down. If she goes public, we can counter with—"

Iva laid a hand on her arm to stop her. "I'm not worried about the business. She can't know all that much, and we'll survive. I'm worried more about you and your relationship with your parents."

"I'm not. I'm more worried about us. You and me."

"We'll be okay, Chey. We just need more time."

"Do we?" She took a deep breath and plunged in. "Dax gave us an early wedding present–open-ended plane tickets and the use of her condo in Hilton Head for a week." Her voice held a note of hope. "We can elope, Iva. Now, today. Just the two of us."

"Wait, what?" Iva's eyes darted back and forth as she took in the information. "Elope? Chey, that's... I don't know if I can do that."

"Why not?" Cheyenne demanded, frustration bubbling up. "Wouldn't it be better than dealing with Sonia Steele or my parents?"

"Maybe. But it's still running away, Chey. We have to face our problems, not run from them. "Anyway," she said, "we've been talking about slowing things way down. Now you come out with this idea? Are you out of your mind?"

"Fine. Then there's something else I need to come clean about." Cheyenne took a deep breath. Her heart pounded in her chest. "When I walked into Celebrate with Style, I had no idea it was your business, Iva. I swear."

"Really?" Iva crossed her arms, her expression unreadable. "I don't understand. Why did you come in?"

Cheyenne confessed, her voice shaky, "I found out about the weddings in an online forum for lesbian and bi women who were looking to get married but wanted to keep it private. I thought I'd make discreet inquiries and see if it could help me."

"Wait, so you were planning on using our business to..." Iva trailed off, her eyes widening in surprise.

"Originally, I was going to tell my parents that I was asking you to marry me just to get them off my back for a while. I knew my father wouldn't approve that you were a woman, but I also figured he'd eventually be happy I was settling down." Cheyenne winced at the memory. "But when I saw you behind the counter, I dropped that plan immediately. I had no idea your business was connected to what I found online."

"Wow." Iva shook her head, trying to process the information. "So you didn't have any romantic intentions or even intend to ask me to be a part of your scheme when you first walked in? You were just going to use me to appease your parents?"

"None," Cheyenne admitted, feeling the heat rise in her cheeks. "I came in with one plan and walked out with a different one."

"I know this must seem so wrong," she said, avoiding Iva's gaze, "but I was going to plan a fake wedding to you and present it to my family without you knowing about it at all. Then, if things didn't work out, I was going to break it off with you and let my family know we had split, and the wedding was off. I figured I'd tell them we were both just too busy to make it work."

Cheyenne paused, finally mustering the courage to look into Iva's eyes. What she saw there almost made her gasp. Iva's face was unreadable, composed in a careful mask.

"I had no idea it was your business I contacted," Cheyenne repeated as she stumbled along with her confession, her voice shaking. "I mean, it's the one time in my life I didn't do my research...my...my journalistic due diligence. I just thought it was so perfect because..."

Her voice trailed off as Iva got up and started walking away. She left the brownstone, her own home.

"Iva!" Cheyenne called out as she went through the front door, but the other woman didn't turn around. She just kept walking, her steps measured and purposeful.

Cheyenne ran to her. When she caught up, she said, "Iva, I'm sorry."

"Sorry?" Iva was incensed that she was going to be used. "What were you planning to tell me? Nothing? Were you going to keep me from ever seeing your family again, afraid if you told me, I'd say something or mess up your plans? I went along with your plan, remember?"

Iva spun on her heel and headed back toward her home. Cheyenne followed, but stopped when Iva whirled on her and laid into her again.

Iva stabbed a finger toward the shop. "That's my business. My livelihood. Mine and Jon's. Now we have people breathing down our necks wanting to take it all away from us, and people like you that are one reason why."

"I'm not doing anymore fake weddings, Cheyenne," Iva ground out, her tone barely above a whisper. "Mine or anyone else's. I'm only doing real ones. Period. I'm not compromising my principals, my integrity anymore."

Cheyenne simply nodded, then she turned and walked away.

No matter what I did, I was going to be damned. The problem is, I really have feelings for Iva and I blew it big time. I should have walked into that shop and played it off months ago when I realized it was Iva's shop. Dropped my plan completely. Said instead that I looked her up because I had to see her. Started a relationship the old-fashioned way. What am I doing, a thirty-four-year-old woman trying to please her

family, and especially her father, anyway? I need to make this right. I need Iva.

"God, I'm such an idiot," Cheyenne mumbled to herself, wiping her eyes with the back of her hand. "I didn't realize how much I loved her until I lost her."

As she walked slowly toward her own brownstone, Cheyenne couldn't help but feel the weight of the world crushing her. The last thing she wanted was to lose not only Iva but also the chance at happiness they could have had together.

"Maybe I should just pack my bags and start over," Cheyenne thought, her heart heavy with despair. "But can I really walk away from her?"

Her footsteps echoed through the nearly deserted streets as tears streamed down her face, blurring her vision. The chill of the evening air did little to cool the burning ache in her chest. She was so consumed by her thoughts that she almost didn't notice Jon standing at his front door, a concerned expression on his face.

"Cheyenne!" he called out, waving her over. "Come in for a bit. It's freezing out here."

She hesitated, wiping away her tears with the back of her hand before crossing the street and stepping into the warm and inviting home Jon shared with Nathan. A delicious smell wafted from the kitchen where Nathan stood, stirring a pot of something that made Cheyenne's stomach grumble.

"Have a seat, darling," Jon said, guiding her to the living room. "You look like you could use a friendly ear."

Perching on the edge of the couch, Cheyenne sniffled and tried to regain her composure. Jon handed her a tissue, which she accepted gratefully. "I just don't know what to do, Jon," she confessed, feeling her voice crack. "I think I've screwed everything up with Iva."

"Let's start from the beginning, honey," Nathan suggested, coming in from the kitchen and joining them. "What happened?"

With a deep breath, Cheyenne recounted the events leading up to her current emotional state - her growing feelings for Iva, their plan to save the business, the elopement idea, and all the disastrous fallout that had followed. As she spoke, she couldn't help but reveal her innermost desires and motivations behind her actions.

"I just wanted to make her happy, you know?" Cheyenne said, her voice barely above a whisper. "But every time I try, I feel like I'm only pushing her further away."

"Sweetie, love is complicated," Jon said, his tone empathetic. "That you're willing to put yourself out there and try says a lot about how much you care for her."

"Besides," Nathan chimed in, "Iva's stronger than you give her credit for. She'll bounce back, and you two can work through this together."

"Really?" Cheyenne asked, hope flickering in her eyes.

"Absolutely," Jon replied with a reassuring smile. "Now, I think it's time we take matters into our own hands to help that along and help you get your girl back."

"Wait, what do you mean?" Cheyenne asked, her curiosity piqued.

"Leave that to us," Nathan said with a wink. "Just trust that we've got your back, and everything will work out."

As they hatched their plan and Cheyenne looked on, watching and listening, she felt a spark of hope ignited within her. Maybe, just maybe, she hadn't lost Iva forever. And with Jon and Nathan by her side, she knew she had the support she needed to make things right.

Cheyenne stared at the flickering candle on the coffee table, a sense of comfort washing over her as she sat between Jon and Nathan. The warm glow cast shadows on their faces, making the room feel intimate and safe.

"Ya know," Jon began, sipping his wine. "Nathan and I didn't have an easy go of it either when we first got together."

"Really?" Cheyenne asked, surprised. She peered at them sitting side by side, holding hands, and saw nothing but the epitome of a perfect couple.

"Yep," Nathan confirmed, nodding as he took Jon's hand. "We met online, which was still pretty unconventional back then. My family wasn't too thrilled about it, and neither were Jon's friends."

"Let's just say there was some... resistance," Jon added, rolling his eyes dramatically. "But we knew what we had was special, and we fought to be together. And look at us now–married and fabulous!"

"Exactly," Nathan chimed in. "The point is, sometimes you have to push through the obstacles to get to the good stuff. Don't give up on love, Chey. Fight for it."

Cheyenne felt a surge of determination and inspiration rushing through her veins. They were right; she couldn't just let Iva slip through her fingers without a fight.

"Speaking of fighting for love," Cheyenne said, a mischievous glint in her eyes. "Add this to your planning and scheming to help me. My sister, Daks we call her–short for Dakota–made me an offer I can't refuse. She's offered plane tickets and the use of her condo in Hilton Head so Iva and I could elope like I told you about."

"Hilton Head? As in, South Carolina?" Jon asked, his eyebrows shooting up in surprise. "Well, that's certainly a romantic destination. I don't know how gay friendly, though."

"It's a really nice condo–beach house, actually–in a nice area on South Beach with its own private beach access. I was down there once, a few years ago." Cheyenne replied, grinning. "I mean, if we're going to elope, we might as well do it somewhere fabulous."

"Absolutely," Nathan agreed, raising his wineglass in a toast. "To love, and to not giving up on the ones who make our hearts sing."

"Cheers to that!" Cheyenne exclaimed, clinking her glass with theirs.

As the laughter echoed through the room, Cheyenne felt a newfound sense of resolve settling within her. With Jon and Nathan's support, she would fight for her love, for Iva. And maybe, just maybe, they'd come out stronger on the other side.

"One thing," Jon said. "The wheels are still turning in my head. What are the marriage rules in South Carolina?"

Cheyenne spread her hands. "Meaning what?"

"There may be a waiting period after you can get a license. That sort of thing."

Nathan grabbed his phone as he volunteered to look it up. It didn't take him long to find something. "You have to apply at a county courthouse," he said, "and there's a twenty-four-hour waiting period before you can officially marry, no exceptions."

"That's not so bad," Cheyenne said.

"Too much can go wrong...like cold feet," Jon said. "Too risky." All was quiet for a minute until Jon clapped his hands together, a grin spreading across his face. "Daks' offer is absolutely brilliant–and I have the perfect solution for your dilemma."

"Really?" Cheyenne asked skeptically, eyeing him as he practically bounced in his seat with excitement.

"Absolutely," Jon confirmed, waving his hand dismissively. "Philly is just the place to be for spur-of-the-moment weddings. Trust me, it's so much easier to get married here than just about anywhere, and I know just the person to help; a justice of the peace who owes me a favor or two."

"Wait, really?" Cheyenne couldn't help but laugh at the unexpected turn of events. If anyone could make this happen, it was Jon.

"Of course! I mean, Iva and I once planned an entire wedding in three days flat–" Jon paused, winking at Cheyenne, "–and it was fabulous, if I may say so myself. So why not take advantage of my connections?"

"Wow, Jon, I don't know what to say." Cheyenne ran a hand through her sandy brown hair, feeling a mix of gratitude and disbelief. "But are you sure about this? It's a lot to ask."

"Please," Jon scoffed, waving her concerns away. "What are friends for? Besides, if I get to plan a whirlwind elopement for the woman I love like a sister and her fiery journalist girlfriend, well, let's just say that's the kind of drama I live for."

Cheyenne chuckled, knowing that Jon wasn't exaggerating in the slightest. "Alright then, let's do this. Let's elope right here in Philly."

"Fantastic!" Jon clapped his hands again, already pulling out his phone to make arrangements. "Leave everything to me–I'll have your license applied for and this wedding planned faster than you can say 'I do.'"

As Jon launched into a flurry of calls and texts, Cheyenne couldn't help but feel the weight of her decision. She was really going to do this—fight for Iva, the woman she loved, in the most unexpected way possible.

"Hey, Jon?" Cheyenne ventured hesitantly, watching as he expertly juggled multiple conversations at once.

"Yep?" Jon replied, pausing just long enough to flash her an encouraging smile.

"Thanks," she said simply, the gratitude clear in her eyes. "For everything."

"Anytime," Jon answered, his voice softer now. "Now go pull yourself together, Chey. Meet me back here at 8:55 AM sharp. We'll get your girl and make this elopement one for the books."

Chapter 22 - Marry Me Now?

♥

Iva Romano sat on the edge of her bed, her hands clasped tightly in her lap, as Cuddles brushed against her leg. A wave of emotions threatened to drown her. The feelings she had for Cheyenne Moore were a whirlwind that left her breathless. She'd never imagined falling so hard for the tomboyish, sandy-haired journalist who lived life out loud.

"Damn it, Chey," Iva whispered to herself. "Why did you have to be so damn...perfect?"

Her thoughts turned to the event planning business she shared with her best friend and confidante. Their plan to stage a fake marriage between her and Cheyenne had ironically been meant to help grow the business legitimately, but now all Iva could think about was how their plan might have done more harm than good.

"Jon's going to kill me," she muttered, burying her face in her hands. "I've ruined everything."

Iva stepped to the door, dreading going outside and dreading going to work. She never dreaded her work. It was a first for her.

Cuddles circled her ankles like she sensed her owner's sadness. Iva bent and gave the cat a scratch along her back, then straightened and stepped out into the bright sunshine of the mid-September morning. *Off to work I go. Other people still have dreams to make reality.*

"Jon, I'm not sure I can do this," Cheyenne admitted, her hands shaking as she clutched the marriage license in front of her. The weight of the decision to ask Iva again to elope was settling in, and doubt crept into her mind.

"Hey," Jon said softly, placing a gentle hand on her shoulder. "You've got this. You love Iva, and I know she loves you, too. Trust yourself."

"Besides," chimed in Nathan, who had been quietly observing from the sidelines, "you've already come this far. And we'll be here every step of the way to support you."

Cheyenne glanced at the two men who had quickly become her confidants and allies in this whirlwind plan. Something about their unwavering faith in her helped chase away some of her doubts. Taking a deep breath, she nodded.

"Okay. Let's do this." She squared her shoulders and smiled determinedly. "Hopeful and determined–that's how we're doing this."

"Damn right," agreed Jon, his own grin contagious. "Now, let's go find your soon-to-be wife."

As they made their way down the block to Iva's brownstone, Cheyenne's nerves returned with a vengeance. Her thoughts raced with potential outcomes and worries for their future. But each time, the memory of Jon and Nathan's encouragement helped center her.

"Remember," Jon whispered as they reached the door, "just be honest with her. That's all any of us can do for love."

"Chey?" Iva asked, her voice quivering. "What are you doing here?" She eyed Jon and Nathan hanging back.

"Hey, Iva," Cheyenne responded softly, searching for the right words. "We need to talk."

"Is this about the business?" Iva's expression flickered to Jon, worry clearly etched there. "I know things have been rough lately, but—"

"No, Iva," Cheyenne interrupted gently. "This is about us."

"Us?"

Cheyenne took a deep breath and launched into her prepared speech. "Iva, I love you. I'm sorry about not being truthful with you. I apologize. None of that changes the fact that I want to spend the rest of my life with you, no matter what that looks like."

Iva stared at her in shock, tears welling up in her eyes once more. "Chey, I–"

"Wait," Cheyenne said, pulling out the marriage license and showing it to Iva. "I've arranged for us to elope in Philly, if you're willing. Jon helped me set everything up. Jon and Nathan. We can do it today. This morning."

Iva looked from the license to Cheyenne's hopeful face, her own expression a mixture of disbelief and joy. "You really did all this for us?"

"Of course," Cheyenne replied, her voice breaking slightly. "Because I can't imagine a future without you."

"Then let's not waste another second," Iva whispered, pulling Cheyenne in for a tearful kiss. "Let's go get married."

Iva smoothed down the simple white sundress she'd selected to wear over the wedding dress she'd originally chosen during their planning phase. She could barely contain her excitement. After all the drama with their families, with Sonia, and over her own fears, she and Cheyenne were doing it, anyway. They were getting married!

Cheyenne fidgeted nervously with her pale blue button-down shirt, having opted for slacks instead of the dress they'd picked for her weeks earlier. She was more comfortable in the pants than she would have ever been in a dress. The dress had been a nod to her family, especially her father. Her sister Daks helped adjust her collar, reassuring her all would be perfect.

Jon flitted about the shop, draping tulle here and hanging flowers there until the place looked like a storybook wonderland. "Only the best for my ladies!" he declared.

His husband, Nathan, just shook his head affectionately at Jon's antics, content to let him work his magic, transforming the shop into a wedding venue.

Just before 11:00 AM, the officiant arrived, slightly bewildered at performing a wedding in a place bursting with party and bridal paraphernalia. "Are you certain this is the correct address?" he asked uncertainly.

"Absolutely!" Jon said. "We're keeping this wedding small and intimate. What better place than an event planning shop that specializes in weddings!"

The officiant, a justice of the peace and longtime friend of Jon's family, still looked puzzled, but obligingly took his place between the makeshift altar they had set up between tables displaying tableware and centerpieces.

Cheyenne and Iva took their places across from him, clasping hands and exchanging nervous glances. This was really happening!

Daks stood as Cheyenne's maid of honor while Jon and Nathan served as Iva's "bridesmen."

As the ceremony began, Jon loudly blew his nose into a monogrammed handkerchief, overcome with emotion. "My little girls are getting married!" he sniffled.

Nathan gently patted his back, a bemused smile on his face. "Easy now, darling. You know how you get with weddings."

A timer buzzed. "The cupcakes!" Daks glanced at her cell phone and gasped. She sprinted away and up the stairs to the kitchen of the small banquet hall on the second-floor mid-ceremony to rescue the desserts from burning.

Cheyenne bit her lip to keep from laughing. Only Daks would bake during her sister's wedding!

After rescuing the cupcakes, Daks scurried back, slightly singed and swearing under her breath. "Please proceed!" she told the baffled officiant.

Suppressing smiles, Iva and Cheyenne recited their vows, meaningful words spoken from the heart. They kept having to pause and wait for Jon's sniffling to subside.

Nathan maintained a straight face but slyly passed Jon tissues and throat lozenges. "Weddings always set him off," he whispered. "Don't know how he makes it in this business."

Finally, it came time for the ring exchange. Daks's eyes widened. "Rings!" She quickly set down the tray of cupcakes she'd been holding and patted her suit jacket pockets in a panic, even though she knew they were empty. She shot a look at Jon who was standing, tissue poised in mid-air, staring back at her.

Seeing her sister's distress, Cheyenne took Iva's hand and quickly removed two beaded bracelets Iva was wearing from her wrist. "Here, these will work."

With a look of relief, Daks handed the makeshift rings over and took her place again.

Iva and Cheyenne held hands, gazing into each other's eyes as they slipped the bracelets on each other.

"With the power vested in me, I now pronounce you married!" the officiant declared. "You may kiss the bride."

Cheyenne and Iva came together in a tender kiss, both blinking back tears. This was really happening!

Daks applauded, Nathan gave a polite golf clap, and Jon dabbed his eyes with a handkerchief.

As they all hugged, Jon cried out, "Wait!" Everyone turned to look at him. "You need to walk back down the aisle together!"

Laughing, Cheyenne and Iva linked arms and made their way between the rows of party gifts, bridal accessories, and all occasions decorations while their friends and family cheered.

Reaching the back of the shop, Cheyenne stopped and turned to Iva. "I can't believe we're finally married," she whispered.

"This is just the start of our lives together," Iva replied, pulling her new wife in for another lingering kiss.

Their joyful union was interrupted by Daks bringing over the slightly burned cupcakes and a container of store-bought frosting for them to share. "Cupcakes first, then kisses!" she said.

After quickly icing and then eating the treats baked with love, it was time for photos. Jon insisted on posing the newlyweds all around the shop. "Give me longing looks by the veils! Show me sultry by the centerpieces!" he directed.

Cheyenne and Iva obliged, having fun with the impromptu wedding photo shoot even if Jon's ideas were unconventional. The joy they felt shone through in every picture.

Later, after changing into casual clothes for their low-key honeymoon, Cheyenne and Iva said their goodbyes. "Thank you both for everything," Iva told Jon and Nathan, hugging them close.

"We're just happy you found each other," Nathan said sincerely. Jon was too choked up to speak, but nodded in agreement.

Daks pulled Cheyenne into a tight hug. "I'm so proud of you," she whispered. "Never let anything come between you again."

Cheyenne hugged her back just as fiercely. "I won't," she promised. Looking over at her glowing bride, she knew she would cherish Iva forever.

After heartfelt hugs and congratulations, Cheyenne and Iva finally departed on their honeymoon getaway, driving off together.

Inside the shop, Jon, Nathan, and Daks stood around the makeshift altar, reflecting on the beautiful, if quirky, wedding they had witnessed.

"Well, that was certainly something," Nathan chuckled, gently nudging a bouquet of fake flowers back into place.

"It was perfect," Daks declared dreamily. "They're meant to be together!"

Jon smiled through his tears. "Our girls chose each other against all odds. You couldn't ask for a happier ending!"

The trio stood in contented silence, surrounded by the wedding decorations bearing witness to the storybook union of Cheyenne and Iva. All was almost right with the world for a time, except for the remains of the slightly burned, slightly off-kilter cupcakes...

Chapter 23 - Honeymooning

♥

Cheyenne carried Iva over the threshold into Daks condo, a beachside bungalow they would stay in for their honeymoon week. She gently set Iva down once inside, both suddenly shy.

"So...here we are," Iva said, fidgeting with her wedding bracelet. This felt strangely more nerve-wracking than their ceremony earlier that day.

"Yeah," Cheyenne laughed awkwardly, running a hand through her hair. She glanced around the dimly lit room, eyes coming to rest on the king-sized bed strewn with pillows. Not exactly how she imagined her wedding night.

Sensing Cheyenne's discomfort, Iva suggested they open a bottle of champagne Daks had, had delivered to the condo and enjoy it on the balcony overlooking the ocean. That would help lighten the mood.

Popping the cork with an impressive spray, Cheyenne poured two bubbly glasses. They clinked them together in a toast; the tension easing slightly.

As the golden liquid fizzed on her tongue, Iva stole glances at her new wife, still hardly believing they had taken such a leap together. It felt surreal.

Cheyenne's thoughts mirrored Iva's. She was still processing that this captivating woman was now her spouse. It was daunting, but she had faith they could make it work.

Finishing their champagne, they stood chatting and looking out at the moonlit waves. Both were reluctant to address the inevitable turn towards physical intimacy.

Iva stifled a yawn. "Well, I don't know about you, but I'm exhausted," she said, hoping Cheyenne would agree sleep was the best choice for tonight.

"Oh yeah, completely wiped out," Cheyenne readily agreed, relief clear in her voice. Sleeping was much more appealing than attempting any awkward intimacy.

After brushing their teeth side-by-side, they crawled onto the massive bed, sticking to their respective edges like opposite poles of a magnet.

Cheyenne fussed with several of the decorative pillows while Iva adjusted and re-adjusted the sheets, both trying to get comfortable.

"Well, goodnight," Iva offered softly, keeping a polite distance. This wasn't exactly a storybook wedding night, but that was okay. They had time.

"Yeah, night," Cheyenne murmured back. She closed her eyes, equally content to just sleep next to Iva, with no forced physicality between them yet.

As the moon cast soft beams across their bed, and the tide sang a nighttime lullaby, the new wives gradually relaxed and drifted off to sleep. There would be no consummation tonight, and they were both perfectly fine with that.

The next morning, soft kisses and shy smiles were exchanged, the initial awkwardness gone. They laughed about their unconventional first night as a married couple over fresh fruit and coffee on the deck overlooking the sea.

"I'm glad we're taking things slow," Iva admitted, squeezing Cheyenne's hand. This felt right for where they were at.

"Me too," Cheyenne agreed readily. "Let's just enjoy being together, no pressure."

They spent the day strolling along the beach hand-in-hand, talking and trading stories about their lives. Learning more about each other.

Later, they shared a romantic candlelit dinner on the beach, feeding each other bites of food and laughing together. All earlier awkwardness had vanished.

When they retreated to the cabana, both were tired again. But this time, Cheyenne shyly invited Iva closer, into her arms.

Iva happily nestled against Cheyenne, resting her head on her chest and listening to the soothing rhythm of her heartbeat.

Cheyenne gently stroked Iva's hair until they both drifted off, feeling closer than the night before, wanting to savor each step they took.

2nd *Full Day*

The morning sun filtered into the beachside bungalow, casting everything in a warm golden glow. Iva rolled over and smiled at the sight of Cheyenne still fast asleep beside her, looking more peaceful than Iva had ever seen her. She almost hated to wake her new wife, but they had plans to go hiking that morning through a forest preserve and then to see the Hilton Head Lighthouse up close.

"Rise and shine, sleepyhead," Iva said softly, brushing a strand of hair back from Cheyenne's face.

Cheyenne scrunched her face adorably and pulled a pillow over her head. "Five more minutes," she mumbled.

Iva laughed and tugged the pillow away. "Come on, the forest preserve, and the lighthouse await! I'll make coffee."

That did the trick. Cheyenne sat up, rubbing the sleep from her eyes. "Coffee first, then hiking."

Soon they were sipping strong coffee on the bungalow's back porch, looking out at the lush greenery beyond, a stark contrast to the wide swath of sand and endless ocean visible from the front deck of the bungalow. The past few days had been idyllic, like a dream come true. They still had so much to learn about each other, but Iva already felt closer to Cheyenne than she had ever felt with anyone.

"What's going on in that head of yours?" Cheyenne asked, noticing Iva's pensive expression.

"Oh, nothing much," Iva said lightly. "Just thinking about how nice this has been. Part of me wishes it didn't have to end."

Cheyenne reached for her hand, giving it a gentle squeeze. "It's only the beginning. We have our whole lives ahead of us."

The certainty in her voice made Iva's heart flutter. "You're right. I guess I'm just sad we'll have to leave this little paradise."

"Me too," Cheyenne sighed, looking around. "But we'll carry it with us. And someday, hopefully, we can build a place of our own that feels just like this."

Iva smiled wistfully. "That would be amazing. As much as I enjoy being in the city, I'm not sure I want to stay in my brownstone long term. Too many memories, good and bad."

Cheyenne nodded in understanding. She understood losing her parents when she was so young had left deep scars for Iva. The brownstone held those ghosts.

"Tell me something about your life before all this craziness. What's the whole story behind that beautiful brownstone of yours?"

Iva's expression softened, and she hesitated for a moment before beginning. "I only told you part of the story before. It...it belonged to my parents before they passed away. My mom was an artist, and she loved every inch of that place. After they were gone, I couldn't bring myself to leave. It was like a part of them lived on within those walls."

"Is that why you've been so hesitant to sell it?" Cheyenne asked gently, her hand finding Iva's and giving it a reassuring squeeze.

"Partly," Iva admitted. "But also, it's been my safe haven, my little corner of the world where I can hide away when everything else gets too overwhelming." She let out a shaky breath, the weight of her confession hanging in the air. "I guess I've always been afraid that if I let it go, I'd lose them all over again."

"Hey," Cheyenne said softly, brushing a stray tear from Iva's cheek. "You're not losing anything. You're simply making space for new memories—ones we'll create together."

"Promise?" Iva whispered, vulnerability shining through her dark eyes. "That's what I thought with Terri. She lived there with me for over two years. Looking back, the poor memories there center on her."

"We can start fresh in my place if you like, for now," Cheyenne suggested. "It's not as big as yours, but big enough for two and your cat. We can take our time finding the perfect place for us. Maybe even build a place, someday."

Iva leaned her head on Cheyenne's shoulder, comforted by the idea of finding or building a home together. "I'd like that. I can't speak for Cuddles, though. Maybe you should break it to her."

After their hike through the forest preserve and a picnic lunch on the beach with a clear view of the famous lighthouse, they returned to the bungalow to escape the afternoon heat. Settling together on the couch, Cheyenne brought up something that had clearly been on her mind.

"Iva, I think once we're back, we should tell our families the truth about how we met and the...unconventional start to our relationship."

Iva tensed slightly. She appreciated Cheyenne's honesty, but the idea of revealing their duplicity made her anxious.

"I agree, but I'm worried about their reactions," she admitted. "Your dad is already angry. What if he sees this as confirmation that it was all a sham to start with and he thinks it still is?"

Cheyenne looked thoughtful. "I think if we explain it right, he'll understand. We can tell him we gave up on an actual wedding and eloped because we wanted to explore our connection with no pressure or judgment." She took Iva's hands in her own. "The important thing is, what started as pretend became very real. We can't change the past, only move forward honestly."

Iva knew Cheyenne was right. Living a lie would only undermine their relationship. And yet...

"It's risky," Iva said slowly. "Your family might feel betrayed."

"They might," Cheyenne acknowledged. "But I'm willing to take that chance, if you are. All that matters to me now is you, Iva. We have to trust our love can withstand the truth."

Iva gazed into Cheyenne's earnest eyes and felt her anxiety melting away. With Cheyenne by her side, she could face anything.

"Okay," Iva said softly. "Together, we'll tell them the whole story. We'll tell Nonna Lena, too. No more secrets."

Cheyenne let out a relieved breath and pulled Iva into a fierce embrace. They stayed that way for a long moment, drawing strength from each other.

"Whatever happens, we're in this together now," Cheyenne murmured against Iva's hair.

Iva clung to her tightly, knowing it was true. Their future path was uncertain, but she was committed, and she knew Cheyenne was too.

That night, under a canopy of stars, Cheyenne led Iva to a secluded spot she had discovered the first time she'd been with her sister and her family to the bungalow—a small hidden cove where the waves lapped gently at the sand.

"Wow, Chey," Iva whispered in awe as they settled onto a blanket spread out on the beach. "This is perfect."

"Only the best for my girl," Cheyenne replied softly, her eyes reflecting the moonlight as she gazed into Iva's.

Their lips met, the passion between them igniting like a slow-burning flame. As they explored each other's bodies, their connection transcended the physical realm, growing into something deeper, more profound than either had ever felt before.

"Chey," Iva murmured, her voice trembling with emotion. "I never thought I could feel this way again."

"Neither did I," Cheyenne admitted, her own vulnerability shining through. "But now that I've found you, Iva, I never want to let go."

"Me neither," Iva agreed, her fingers entwining with Cheyenne's. "We'll make it work, no matter what."

"Damn right, we will," Cheyenne vowed, sealing the promise with another tender kiss.

As the waves continued to ebb and flow around them, Cheyenne and Iva sank into the soft sand and surrendered themselves to the moment.

Iva felt like she and Cheyenne were the only ones in the world, and she wanted to savor the moment. She looked over at Cheyenne, lying beside her, hair tousled by the gentle breeze. In that moment, Iva felt an overwhelming love and tenderness towards her wife.

She got closer to Cheyenne and caught her face in her hands. She looked deep into Cheyenne's eyes and saw the love that was radiating out from within.

Their kiss was passionate, like a storm of emotion and sensation. Iva's hands slipped down to grip Cheyenne's body as she became lost in a whirlwind of feeling and desire. Iva felt an ever-increasing heat within her as the kiss grew more and more passionate.

Cheyenne's hands slid around Iva's waist and pulled her closer, their lips pressing together as if they could never be apart. Iva felt like time had stopped and that the only thing that mattered was the love they were sharing at that moment.

The waves seemed to whisper in the background, adding a gentle ambiance to their embrace. Iva and Cheyenne lolled on the sand, oblivious to the world around them.

Eventually, Cheyenne broke away, her eyes twinkling with joy. She grabbed Iva's hand, pulled her to her feet, and led her towards the sea. Iva felt a tingle of excitement as they walked together, her long coverup dress flowing in the breeze.

As they reached the water's edge, Cheyenne turned and faced Iva. She placed her hands on Iva's hips and leaned in for another kiss. This time, the kiss was more tender, like a whisper of love and devotion. Iva could feel her heart pounding in her chest as the kiss lingered.

Cheyenne removed Iva's thin beach coverup, slowly revealing her body, clad only in a bikini beneath. After Cheyenne helped her out of that too, Iva felt vulnerable and exposed, yet strangely safe in Cheyenne's arms. She followed suit, undressing Cheyenne with her hands and eyes.

The two stood facing each other, naked and unashamed. Iva ran her hands over Cheyenne's body, feeling the contours of her skin, the curves of her muscles, and the warmth of her embrace. Cheyenne did the same, spreading kisses across Iva's neck, shoulders, and chest.

Finally, they stepped into the shallow sea and embraced each other in a warm embrace. The waves lapped around them, embracing them as their bodies moved in a slow, graceful dance. They were lost in a world of pleasure, and every cell in their bodies seemed to sing with joy.

Iva and Cheyenne moved as one, exploring each other's bodies, kissing, and caressing. They melted into one another, their bodies connecting that felt like a dream.

Iva smiled as she felt Cheyenne's touch. It was like nothing she had ever experienced before. There was a sense of intimacy in their lovemaking that she had never felt with anyone else. It was more than just passion. It was a communion of souls, a mutual exchange of emotions and energy.

The waves washed over Iva, cooling her as she felt her desire growing more and more intense. She looked over and saw Cheyenne's eyes ablaze with passion, and an overwhelming feeling of love washed over her.

Cheyenne swept Iva up in her arms and carried her to the shore. She laid her on the soft, wet sand and began her sensual assault.

Iva's body was wracked with waves of pleasure as Cheyenne's tongue explored every inch of her breasts. She felt her heart pound as she savored every touch, every caress.

Iva's hands roamed Chey's body as she kissed her neck, her breasts, and moved her inner thighs. She could feel her desire growing and knew that she wanted to give all of herself to Cheyenne.

Iva pulled Chey up to kiss her, wrapping her arms around her and pulling her in close. She was lost in a sea of desire, a place where there was nothing but pleasure. She felt Cheyenne's heart beating in her chest, and she bent to kiss it passionately.

Cheyenne broke away and Iva could see the passion burning in her eyes, too. She felt the heat of Cheyenne's body as she pulled back for a moment. Chey's hips moved against her, sending shockwaves of desire through her body.

She felt Cheyenne's body move lower, and then her tongue was all over her, licking and teasing, penetrating and stimulating. Iva moaned as she felt her desire growing ever stronger.

Cheyenne's hands slid over Iva's body, feeling her curves, her softness, her passion. Her tongue continued to work its magic, sending waves of pleasure through Iva's body.

"Cheyenne!" Iva moaned. Her body seemed to be aflame with desire, a fire that only Cheyenne could quench. She felt her hips buck up to meet Cheyenne's mouth, driving her tongue deeper and deeper. She felt a sense of overpowering pleasure overtake her body, and she writhed on the sand.

Iva felt Cheyenne's hand slide into her, massaging and caressing her, and her desire built to a fevered pitch. Iva moaned, her voice echoing in the waves. Her body felt like it was going to explode, and then she felt Cheyenne's tongue circle her clit as her fingers stroked deeper.

Iva felt a wave of pleasure spread through her body, coming out of the most intense orgasm of her life. She screamed Cheyenne's name, and Cheyenne collapsed on top of her, exhausted. The waves lapped over them as they lay there, panting for breath.

Cheyenne and Iva stumbled into the bungalow, laughing in disbelief at how long it had taken them to make love.

"We should have done this ages ago!" Iva said, her face flushed with pleasure.

"I know, right? It was amazing!" Cheyenne replied breathlessly.

Covered in sand, they collapsed onto the floor, still shaking with pleasure from their passionate encounter on the beach.

"It was worth the wait!" Iva said, a contented smile spreading across her face.

Cheyenne nodded in agreement. "It certainly was! We should do it more often."

"How about a shower?" Iva asked.

Chey quirked an eyebrow. "You're asking me to shower with you? So soon?"

"I have a few things I'd like to do to you, but first, the sand has to go."

"Alrighty, then. Bold. I like it. Looks good on you," Chey teased.

The warm, salty breeze danced through the open windows of their beachfront bungalow as Cheyenne and Iva enjoyed their last morning in their honeymoon paradise. They took their coffee to the deck, but Cheyenne couldn't stay out of the sand for long.

"I'm going to miss this," Cheyenne sighed, as she stepped off the low deck, kicked off her sandals and stretched out on the sand on a beach towel. "Nothing beats the feeling of sand between your toes."

"Speak for yourself," Iva retorted playfully, eyeing the invasive grains and recalling their lovemaking in it the night before. "I'm more of a city girl myself." She sat down next to Cheyenne, a mischievous glint in her eyes. "But I suppose I could get used to this... for a week at a time or so."

"Give it time," Cheyenne replied, turning her head to plant a lingering kiss on Iva's lips. "You'll fall in love with this place just like you did with me."

"Bold assumption," Iva teased, though her cheeks flushed from the compliment.

"Hey, I'm a risk-taker," Cheyenne said, grinning. "And speaking of risks, how about we rent some scooters and explore the rest of the island today?"

"Is that really a risk or just an excuse to show off your driving skills?" Iva shot back, but her smile betrayed her enthusiasm.

"Both," Cheyenne admitted with a laugh, pulling Iva closer. "Remember the surrey bike?"

"What are you trying to say? I'm a poor driver?"

"No, no," Cheyenne backtracked. "Not at all."

"I drive the Celebrate with Style van all the time. I've never had an accident."

"Does Jon ride with you?"

"Why?"

Cheyenne shrugged. "Just curious.

"Jon has a license, but he prefers not to drive."

"I see."

"I'm a good driver, Chey."

Cheyenne laughed as she raised her hands in mock surrender. "Okay. You'll get to show me today."

"You're on, Moore!"

They both looked at each other then. Iva broke the silence first. "That's something we haven't talked about, Chey."

"Names? Yeah, I never thought about it until just now."

"You're pretty well known as Cheyenne Moore what with your bylines and all. I wouldn't want you to change."

"And you're a Romano from the tippy-top of your raven haired head to the tips of your bright red toenails. I wouldn't want you to change that either."

"Hyphenate?" Iva asked. They both shook their heads no.

"Let's do this. We keep our names," Cheyenne said, "but we up our wedding band game." She fingered the bracelet on her wrist for effect.

"Deal. Do you want to shop here on the island, today?"

"Only if we can find rings we like we can wear home tomorrow. Otherwise, let's do it in Philly."

Iva said, "If we don't find something today, I know the perfect place...but I really would like to look today."

"Let's get moving then, woman. We're wasting daylight."

Chapter 24 - Coming Clean

♥

Cheyenne's heart raced as she stared at the wedding band on her finger, a symbol of the web of lies that had entangled her and Iva.

As they climbed into Daks' SUV, tension hung heavy in the air like a dense fog. Cheyenne fiddled with the seatbelt, her fingers trembling with anxiety, while Iva chewed on her lower lip. Jon, seated next to Iva, glanced back and forth between his best friend and Cheyenne, sensing their unease.

"Hey, you two," he said with an exaggerated grin, trying to lighten the mood. "What's the deal? Did someone forget to laugh at my last joke or something?"

"Very funny, Jon," Cheyenne responded, forcing a smile. "We're just... working through some stuff. That's all."

"Ah, I see," Jon said, nodding knowingly. "Well, in that case, maybe I can help take your minds off of it with a little game." He pulled out his phone and tapped the screen a few times. "How about some good old-fashioned 'Would You Rather?'"

"Jon, I'm not really in the mood for—" Cheyenne began, but he cut her off.

"Come on, just one round," he cajoled. "I promise, it'll be fun!"

"Fine," she relented, exchanging a look with Iva, who shrugged and nodded agreement.

"Alright!" Jon exclaimed, his face lighting up. "First question: Would you rather have to wear clown shoes every day or a clown wig?"

As they drove toward Cheyenne's family home, Jon continued to toss out absurd questions, eliciting laughter from both Iva and Cheyenne. For a moment, their worries receded into the background. But as the SUV turned onto the familiar street, Cheyenne's stomach churned with dread, knowing she couldn't avoid telling the truth any longer.

The scent of roast chicken and garlic wafted through the air as Cheyenne and Iva entered the dining room. The long wooden table was set with fine china, polished silverware, and an elegant floral centerpiece. Cheyenne's mother had always been an excellent cook, but tonight's meal seemed to be a cut above the rest - an unwitting celebration of the bombshell they were about to drop.

"Ah, there you are, girls!" Thomas greeted them, his booming voice echoing off the high ceiling. He looked up from his seat at the head of the table, his salt-and-pepper eyebrows furrowing in concern as he took in their tense expressions. "You two look like you've seen a ghost. What's going on?"

"Um, Dad," Cheyenne began, her voice wavering slightly. She glanced over at Iva, who offered her a small, encouraging smile. "We... we need to talk to you about something."

"Is everything okay?" Thomas asked, his gaze shifting between his daughter and Iva with growing unease.

"Actually, no," Cheyenne confessed, taking a deep breath. "It's about our engagement. It's... it's not real. Wasn't real. Not at first." She hesitated for a beat, then added, "And we eloped."

Thomas blinked, staring at the pair in disbelief. Then, without warning, his anger erupted like a volcano, his fist slamming down onto the table with such force that the fine china rattled and the water glasses trembled. "What the hell do you mean it wasn't real? And then you eloped?! So the marriage isn't real either?"

Cheyenne flinched at the outburst, feeling her heart race as she fought to maintain her composure. "Dad, please, just let me explain—"

"Explain?!" Thomas roared incredulously. "How could you even think of doing something like this, Cheyenne? And Iva, I thought you had more sense than to go along with it!"

Iva straightened her shoulders, her eyes flashing defiantly. "We never meant for things to get out of hand," she said firmly. "It started as an arrangement of sorts, but then it snowballed, and some things got out of hand...but then we really fell for each other."

"God, I can't believe this!" Thomas exclaimed, his voice heavy with frustration and disappointment. "You two need to fix this mess immediately. I don't care how you do it, but you better make sure everyone knows the truth."

"Of course, Dad," Cheyenne murmured, her cheeks burning with shame. She wanted nothing more than to crawl under the table and hide, but that was impossible. Instead, she forced herself to meet her father's furious gaze, determined to make amends.

"Right," Thomas said, his tone icy and unforgiving. "Get it done."

As Cheyenne and Iva retreated from the dining room, their shoulders sagging beneath the weight of Thomas's anger, they couldn't help but wonder how they would ever untangle themselves from the web of lies they'd woven.

As Cheyenne and Iva stumbled out of the dining room, they found themselves in the hallway, feeling as though the air had been sucked from their lungs. Ruth's quiet sobs reached their ears, like the distant sound of a dying animal, making Cheyenne's heart lurch painfully in her chest.

"Mom," she whispered, turning to see her mother's tear-streaked face. The pain etched into Ruth's expression was almost unbearable, and Cheyenne felt a wave of guilt wash over her.

"Chey, I just don't understand," Ruth choked out between soft sobs. "Why would you do this to us? To yourself?"

"I'm so sorry, Mom," Cheyenne replied, her voice barely audible. "I never meant to hurt anyone."

"Darling, it's not just about the hurt," Ruth said, her voice wavering. "It's the disappointment. We thought we knew you better than this. We thought we'd raised you to be honest and true to yourself."

"Mom, let's take a step back," Daks urged gently, placing a comforting hand on her mother's shoulder. "They know they messed up, and they've apologized. They're very much in love and planning for the future. We all need to figure out how to move forward from here and support them."

"Thank you, Daks," Iva murmured gratefully, casting a sidelong glance at Jon, who was watching the scene unfold with a mixture of concern and sympathy.

"Right," Jon chimed in, clapping his hands together briskly. "We're all adults here, and we know people make mistakes. What's important is that we learn from them and do our best to make amends."

"Jon's right," Daks agreed, nodding firmly. "Cheyenne and Iva have owned up to their mistake, and now it's time for us to help them sort this out."

"Okay," Ruth sniffed, dabbing at her eyes with a tissue. "I just hope we can put this behind us and move on."

"We will, Mom," Cheyenne promised, reaching out to take her mother's hand. "I swear, we'll make it right."

"Let's all sit down together and come up with a plan to tell the rest of the clan," Daks suggested, her tone businesslike but compassionate. "We're a family, and we'll get through this as a family."

"Agreed," Jon added, his usual flamboyance subdued in the face of the emotional turmoil around him. "Together, we can fix this."

As they gathered in the living room, united minus Thomas in their determination to mend the rift that had formed between them, Cheyenne couldn't help but feel a glimmer of hope amid the chaos. They might have made a mess of things, but with the love and support of her mother, she knew they could make amends and move forward. She hoped her father would come around.

Cheyenne pulled open the heavy oak door, the late afternoon sun momentarily blinding her as she stepped outside. She shielded her eyes, blinking to adjust. Behind her, Iva, Jon, and Daks filed out of the Moore family home, the screen door slamming shut behind them.

"Well, that was...something," Jon muttered, smoothing his vest and glancing back at the house apprehensively.

Cheyenne sighed, raking a hand through her hair. "I know Dad means well, but he just doesn't get it sometimes."

"At least Mom's on your side," Daks offered with an encouraging smile, giving Cheyenne's arm a supportive squeeze.

Iva glanced between them, uncharacteristically quiet as she fidgeted with the strap of her purse. Cheyenne made a mental note to check in with her new wife about her thoughts on it all later.

"Right, enough family drama for one day," Jon declared, clapping his hands together decisively. "Let's head downtown and regroup. I texted Nathan and told him to meet us at the La Columbe in..." He checked his watch. "...fifteen minutes ago. Oops."

Daks laughed, leading the way down the front steps. "Well, we better get a move on, then. Don't want to keep him waiting."

The group piled into Daks' SUV, a welcome blast of air conditioning greeting them as they slid into the leather seats. Cheyenne leaned her head back, closing her eyes briefly as her sister pulled away from the curb. She replayed the conversation with her parents in her mind, hoping they'd been able to get through to them. For now, they had bigger fish to fry. Sonia Steele wouldn't know what hit her...

La Columbe was bustling with activity when they arrived, the rich aroma of coffee enveloping them as they stepped inside. Nathan was seated at a table tucked into the back corner, nursing an iced latte as he scrolled through his phone. He glanced up as they approached, breaking into a smile.

"Hey babe," he said, standing to give Jon a quick kiss. "Glad you could make it. I already got your usual."

Jon grinned, picking up the steaming mug. "Have I told you lately that I love you?"

Nathan chuckled. "Maybe once or twice."

They settled around the table; the mood growing serious as they got down to business.

"So what's the plan?" Nathan asked, glancing between them. "How do we take down the infamous Sonia Steele?"

Iva cleared her throat, uncharacteristically nervous. "I've been thinking about that. And I have an idea, but you may not like it."

Cheyenne frowned, leaning forward. She could tell Iva was anxious about proposing something risky. "What is it, Iva? You know we'll support you no matter what."

"I think we need to shut down the fake side of the wedding business," Iva said finally, not quite meeting their eyes. "At least for now. If Sonia tries to come after us legally, it could look terrible if she exposes that side of things."

Nathan's eyebrows shot up in surprise. "Whoa...that's a pretty big step."

Jon bit his lip uncertainly. "I don't know, Iva. That's a big financial hit we'd be taking. And what will we tell our clients?"

Iva sighed, nodding. "I know, I know. But I really think this is the safest option right now. We can't risk Sonia having any more ammunition against us." She looked between them all pleadingly. "I'm open to other ideas, but I don't see another way through this."

Cheyenne hesitated, exchanging a look with Nathan. As much as she hated to admit it, Iva had a point, and she already knew how Iva felt about the morality of it all. If they wanted to take the moral high ground here, they needed to play this carefully.

"Okay," she said finally. "I think you're right. You need to protect yourselves. We'll figure out the money stuff later."

Nathan nodded reluctantly toward Jon. "Alright, I'm with you. Sonia doesn't get to win this round."

Iva's shoulders sagged in relief. "Thank you, both of you. I know this won't be easy, but it's the right thing to do."

Iva, Nathan, Cheyenne, and Daks tossed around some ideas to bring in new, legitimate business.

Jon had been quiet until that point, contemplating Iva's proposal. Finally, he spoke up.

"I think this is the smartest play," he said decisively. Iva looked at him in surprise.

"Really? Even with the financial impact?"

Jon nodded. "Especially because of the financial impact. Let's face it - the fake wedding side of things has always been ethically questionable. The second Sonia threatened us, continuing it became too risky."

He leaned forward, urgency in his voice. "We built this business on creativity and heart, not scams. If shutting down the fake weddings protects that, I say good riddance."

Iva smiled in relief, reaching out to squeeze his hand. "Thank you. I'm glad you're with me on this."

Jon squeezed back. "Always am. Now let's figure out damage control."

The group launched into a lively discussion of contingency plans.

Iva pointed out they'd lose at least a third of their wedding clientele and weddings made up the bulk of their business. "We'll need to cut costs and get creative with new offerings," she mused.

Nathan suggested focusing on smaller, more personal events. Jon proposed virtual consulting sessions. Slowly, ideas took shape for keeping their business afloat while they rebuilt.

Iva nodded along as her friends brainstormed, but her stomach churned. She knew this was the right thing to do, but the potential fallout terrified her.

Finally, she spoke up. "I know this is our best option, but I'm worried. We could lose so much business, and our reputation might take a tremendous hit."

She looked around at her friends' faces, anxiety creeping into her voice. "How will we make up for all that lost revenue? Can we really survive this?"

Jon reached out and put a reassuring hand on her shoulder. "Hey, don't spiral. We've got this."

He leaned in, his voice calm. "Remember when we first started out? We built this from nothing before, and we can do it again. It'll be lean for a bit, but we'll get creative."

Iva took a deep breath, letting his confidence anchor her.

"You're right," she said. "We'll focus on smaller events - the ones that really touch people's hearts. And we'll find new ways to get our services out there. It's time I finally learn social media marketing!"

She laughed, anxiety dissipating.

Daks nodded enthusiastically. "I love that attitude, Iva! And don't worry about marketing - I've got you covered there."

She leaned forward, eyes sparkling with excitement. "Start posting on social media daily, showcase your best events with gorgeous photos, run some targeted ads. I've got nothing but time, so I can help with a lot of that, and Cheyenne here can help me optimize everything when she's not on the road...and even sometimes when she is. She's a genius with that stuff."

Cheyenne rolled her eyes but smiled. "Oh, I don't know about genius, but I'm happy to help however I can."

Nathan chimed in. "I'll pitch in too - I've got a few connections of my own, some strings I can pull."

Jon grinned. "See? We're an unstoppable team. All that's left is making it official."

He looked around at the group. "So, we're decided - we shut down the fake side completely, come clean to Iva's Nonna Lena like with the Moores, and focus on building the real deal. All in favor?"

A chorus of "ayes" echoed around the table.

Iva exhaled, the tension leaving her body. They had a plan. With her friends' support, she could face anything. The future seemed bright again.

"Alright team," Jon said, clapping his hands together. "Let's do this."

Iva nodded, determination steeling her nerves. "Okay, first things first - we need to notify all existing fake clients that we're dissolving their contracts. I'll draft an email explaining we're shifting our business model."

She paused, thinking. "For the real clients, we could offer a discount on their packages as an apology for the deception. That might help smooth things over."

"Good call," Jon said. He frowned slightly. "We should also remove any mention of the fake services from the underground websites where it exists."

"Let me work on that," Cheyenne offered. "I'm pretty good at that sort of digging, in my day job...except for this one time..."

Iva tried to smile, but sighed instead. "This is really happening. It's the right thing to do, but it feels strange dismantling something we built up over years."

Jon squeezed her hand reassuringly. "I know, but it'll be worth it. No more looking over our shoulders waiting for the axe to fall."

He smiled. "Just think - soon it'll be nothing but real brides, real grooms, real cake tastings and flower arrangements. We're going completely legit, Iva!"

Despite her nerves, Iva couldn't help but smile back. The future was uncertain, but she had faith. With Jon, Cheyenne, and her friends by her side, she could weather any storm.

"Onwards and upwards," she said. "I can't wait to see what the future holds for all of us."

The offices of Married with Magic

The atmosphere in the room felt charged with the tension of their argument. Cheyenne, Iva, and Jon had finally owned up to their deception, but Sonia Steele remained unmoved. She stared at them with a mixture of fury and disbelief, her arms crossed tightly across her chest.

"I can't believe what you've done," she said coldly. "Did you ever think how much what you've been up to hurts the whole wedding planning business?"

The three of them exchanged anxious glances.

"We're sorry," Iva said. "We never meant to hurt anyone."

Cheyenne and Jon nodded in agreement.

"We thought we were helping some of those clients," Jon added. "But we understand how wrong it was."

Sonia sighed. She could see that they truly were sorry—even if they had gone about expressing all of it in the wrong way.

"Well," she said, softening her expression as she thought of an appropriate solution. "I suppose I could accept your apology if you promise not to make any more fake wedding arrangements and to refer none of those potential clients to Married with Magic. I don't want the liability."

Jon laughed. "Come on, now," he said. "Not even one?"

Sonia scowled, and the others immediately realized she was still harboring a grudge.

"None," Iva said quickly. "We swear."

Sonia nodded, finally accepting their offer. "Okay," she said. "Let's just forget this all ever happened."

The group exhaled in relief, grateful that the situation had been resolved.

Epilogue

Six months later...

Iva's spirited Nonna Lena fussed over her, insisting on doing her hair herself. "No one can handle these thick Italian locks like me!"

Meanwhile, Cheyenne's sister Daks helped her get dressed, swatting away her hands when she tried to help. "Let me serve my only sister on her big day!"

Daks' young daughter brought Cheyenne her "something blue"–a clumsy homemade card with a lopsided heart. "I made it myself!" she said proudly.

Cheyenne hugged her tightly. "It's perfect. I'll keep it forever." She tucked the card safely in her pocket next to her heart.

In the small banquet hall upstairs from Celebrate with Style, Iva's best friend Jon flitted about, making sure every detail was perfect.

His husband, Nathan, sat stoically in the front row next to Cheyenne's eager mother, Ruth, who kept peering around, expecting Cheyenne's father to show up.

But as the music started, it seemed Thomas was not coming after all. Ruth sighed, saddened but unsurprised by her stubborn husband's absence.

Just as Iva and Cheyenne joined hands at the altar, the door creaked open and Thomas entered silently. Ruth gasped in shock.

The officiant paused, waiting to see if Thomas would object. But he simply sat down without a word, his face unreadable.

Exchanging puzzled glances, Iva and Cheyenne proceeded with their vows. This was their day; Thomas wouldn't ruin it.

After exchanging actual wedding bands and being pronounced wife and wife once more, they kissed sweetly, lost in their own private world of love.

The small gathering erupted into cheers and applause, even the children making delighted noises. Nonna Lena wiped her eyes, overcome with pride.

At the reception, Thomas approached the brides with an uncharacteristic hesitance. "I owe you both an apology," he began somberly.

"When you first married, I refused to believe it was real. I listened to other people and didn't see what was in front of my eyes." His voice was gruff with emotion. "I judged unfairly, and for that I am deeply sorry."

Iva took his hand, smiling gently. "The past is behind us. All is forgiven." Cheyenne slipped her arm around her father, wordlessly reconciling.

Thomas cleared his throat, composing himself. "If you'll permit me, I have a gift." He presented them with the deed to a property just outside the city. "It's a beautiful parcel of land with a small but comfortable house, and plenty of space to build your dream house someday."

"Dad...it's perfect," Cheyenne whispered, tears in her eyes.

"This is incredibly generous," added Iva, squeezing Thomas' hand. His meaningful gesture of acceptance meant everything.

Ruth dabbed her eyes with a tissue as she joined them. "Now we're all one big happy family!" She pulled Thomas into an embrace.

Nearby, in the small room, the children were chasing each other around in a raucous game of tag. "Be careful!" Daks called out futilely.

Nonna Lena cackled with delight as the little ones wove between the tables and chairs, ignoring their mother's pleas. "Let them be. They're celebrating!"

Jon and Nathan entered from the kitchen carrying a lopsided wedding cake they had baked themselves. "It's not perfect, but it's made with love!" Jon said.

Everyone gathered around, oohing and ahhing over the charming cake. Iva and Cheyenne cut the first slice together, smiles radiant with joy. Looking around at their eclectic yet wonderful family, the brides' hearts swelled with gratitude. All were here together now.

"To new beginnings," Cheyenne toasted later, raising her glass.

"And the joining of families," added Iva, clinking their glasses.

As laughter and merry voices filled the room, Iva rested her head on Cheyenne's shoulder with a contented sigh.

Cheyenne pressed a kiss to her hair. "Can you believe this is our life now?"

Iva smiled up at her, pure adoration in her eyes. "I wouldn't change a thing."

Watching the two younger women glow with joy, Iva's Nonna, Lena and Cheyenne's mother Ruth exchanged a knowing look. They had seen the blossoming love from the start.

Now here Cheyenne and Iva stood, surrounded by those they held most dear, their hearts fuller than they could have imagined. The trials they had weathered faded to distant memory. All that remained was a profound gratitude for the family they had found together.

Thomas approached the two family matriarchs, three glasses of champagne in hand. "To the future," he toasted.

"And to love that lasts," Ruth added warmly. Nonna Lena just smiled, her heart too full for words.

Looking around the room, Iva felt tears prick her eyes. Their family was patchwork, imperfect, and absolutely beautiful. It was everything.

She caught Cheyenne's gaze from across the room, love passing silently between them. A perfect, joyful ending to their winding, fake to forever journey.

Afterward

♥

I like to try to give readers insight into the roots of my stories where such roots exist and are not complete figments of my imagination. If you'd like to know a little about how my mind works, read on. If not, skip this part.

Significant pieces of the early part of Iva and Chey's story came to me one night in a dream. The scene where Cheyenne impulsively kisses Iva at the block party and the immediate aftermath where she follows Terri to Iva's brownstone, specifically. I was working on a short story for something else at the time and I thought about working those scenes from my dream into that story, but I soon came to realize Cheyenne deserved her own story.

One of my favorite romantic movies, 'Moonstruck,' starring Cher as Loretta and Nicolas Cage as Ronny, also played out a lot in my mind as I wrote this. True, New York was the setting for that movie, not Philadelphia, but the brownstone, the Italian family dynamics, the humor, the impulsiveness, the turbulence–it's all there. I just made it gay!

In my teen years, I spent some enjoyable time in Philadelphia, one of my first forays into the world sans my family. The city was new, exciting, and intriguing to me in retrospect, as so many things can be that contain fond memories of the past. Looking back, I feel old as those times were just over forty years ago. Since that time, I'd passed through Philly as an adult occasionally, but I hadn't spent significant time there. It was a shame and one I rectified recently with a long weekend trip. It wasn't the city of my memories. Parts were gone, parts should be gone, and other changes have been made that are for the better.

I didn't come from money growing up, as Chey does in this story. My parents scrimped so I could spend that time in Philly. I worked a part-time job after school and saved my money too. I had friends who went to the city with me though who had parents who were, while not wealthy, comfortable and able to send their daughters along with barely a thought about the cost. One fellow traveler, a friend and rival at the time (who, in retrospect, I had a huge crush on) came from a 'comfortable' family. In our senior year in high school, she was dating a boy whose parents were wealthy. He was taking her to Hilton Head for spring break, just the two of them, with her parents' blessing. Times were a lot different then!

My friendly rival regaled us with stories of their time on Hilton Head Island. It's a place I've always wanted to go, as a result, but where I've never been. Yet, I've been so close to it! I spent months in a military school at Fort Gordon, Georgia, near Agusta and spent some time in Savannah, Georgia. I've been to the Marine Corps base at Parris Island...an Island over, but a bit of a convoluted drive away. That part of Iva and Chey's story carries only a tiny resemblance to my friend's stories. Everything about the island I know from the internet. If I've gotten anything wrong, I'm entirely to blame.

About the Author

A nne Hagan is the author of over twenty full-length works of fiction in the mystery, romance, and thriller genres. She writes of family, friends, love, murder, and mayhem in no particular order and often all in the same story. She's a half owner of the weekly discount eBook newsletter, MyLesfic, a wife, parent, foster parent, and an Army veteran. When she writes, she draws from her experiences because truth is often stranger than fiction.

Check Anne Out on the web, on Facebook or on X (Twitter)

For the latest information about upcoming releases, other projects, sample chapters and everything personal, check out Anne's **site** at https://AnneHaganAuthor.com/ or like Anne on **Facebook** at https://www.facebook.com/AuthorAnneHagan. You can also connect with Anne on **Twitter** @AuthorAnneHagan.

Join Anne's email List

♥

Are you interested in **free books**? How about **free short stories**? For those and all the latest news on new releases, **opportunities to get review copies of all of her new releases** and more, please consider joining Anne's email list at: https://www.AnneHaganAuthor.com by filling in the brief form in the sidebar.

Also By

The books of the Morelville Mysteries series Anne's sapphic themed mystery/romance series:

Relic: The Morelville Mysteries–Book 1–The first Dana and Sheriff Mel mystery and the first book in the Morelville saga.
Cases collide for two star crossed ladies of law enforcement!

Busy Bees: The Morelville Mysteries–Book 2
Romance and Murder Mix in the Latest Story Featuring Sheriff Mel Crane and Special Agent Dana Rossi!

Dana's Dilemma: The Morelville Mysteries–Book 3–The relationship matures between Mel and Dana in an installment that features a breaking Amish character, an ex-girlfriend, a conniving politician, and murder.
Elections and Old Loves Combine with Deadly Results in a Romantic Mystery Featuring Sheriff Mel Crane and Special Agent Dana Rossi!

Hitched and Tied: The Morelville Mysteries–Book 4
Mel and Dana attempt to bring their growing romantic relationship
full circle, but family, duty, and family duties all conspire to get in
the way.

Viva Mama Rossi!: The Morelville Mysteries–Book 5–The 5th tale
in the Morelville Mysteries and the book that gives fans a full introduction to future Morelville Cozies series sleuths Faye Crane (Mel's
mom) and Chloe Rossi (Dana's Mama). The two series stand-alone,
but they're certainly better together.
A delayed honeymoon getaway takes a deadly turn for newlyweds
Mel and Dana; meanwhile, two meddling mothers won't let sleeping
fisherman lie in the latest Morelville Mystery.

A Crane Christmas: The Morelville Mysteries–Book 6
Is it the Christmas season or the 'silly season'?

Mad for Mel: The Morelville Mysteries–Book 7
Rival gangs will stop at nothing to gain sole control of the drug
trade in Muskingum County, and they've picked Valentine's week
to create a firestorm of murder and mayhem as they battle each other
for supremacy.

Hannah's Hope: The Morelville Mysteries–Book 8
A young mother with a troubled past seeks help from Mel and Dana, but is their effort to assist her too little, too late?

The Turkey Tussle: The Morelville Mysteries–Book 9
The old-fashioned country village of Morelville holds a secret.

Sullied Sally: The Morelville Mysteries–Book 10
An unsolved murder, over 40 years in the past, leads to the discovery of a new victim and the return of an old stalker.

Finding Sheila: The Morelville Mysteries–Book 11
A woman, imprisoned for manslaughter, disappears without a trace during transport between states, and it's all up to Dana to find her.

Tennessee Bound: The Morelville Mysteries–Book 12
The politics and the paper-pushing are wearing on Sheriff Mel. Will she chuck it all?

A spinoff of Anne's Morelville Mysteries series, The Morelville Cozies series features meddling mother sleuths Faye Crane and Chloe Rossi getting mixed up in mysteries all their own.

The Passed Prop: The Morelville Cozies–Book 1
Chloe Rossi wants to retire with her husband and move away from suburban sprawl to bucolic Morelville; the only trouble is, Morelville is experiencing its worst crime wave ever, and Marco Rossi wants no part of a move there. What to do?

Opera House Ops: The Morelville Cozies–Book 2
Murder and other sinister goings-on at a vacant 1800s era opera house in Morelville and a modern-day property developer who wants to raze the historic building for his own gain have the village residents all tied up in knots and Faye Crane trying to play savior to history.

The Conjuring Commedienne: The Morelville Cozies–Book 3
Faye thinks Hattie's a suspect. Chloe thinks she's a kindred soul. Only Hattie knows for sure!

Anne's Romance Novels and Novellas:

Misfit Christmas – A Colorado Holiday Romance

Broken Women
Can two women, unlucky in love, find solace in each other?

Healing Embrace–The stand-alone sequel to Broken Women
Barb and Janet were a couple... and then they weren't. What now?

Steamboat Reunion–the third and final book in the Barb and Janet
series
Can you go home again?

A Sweetwater Christmas
Traditional and progressive meet in ruby red west-central Texas...
This novella is a significant expansion of the short story, Loving Blue
in Red States: Sweetwater Texas.

Christmas Cakes and Kisses
Two different worlds brought together by cake...

Steel City Confidential–Anne's first legal thriller (AKA The Thelma and Louise Book)
Clients hide things from their lawyers all the time. Pam Wilson makes it an art form.

Published Short Stories

Series and Collections:

Loving Blue in Red States
A sapphic romance *short story* series that kicks off with a visit to the little town of Sweetwater, Texas. It's followed by stops in Birmingham, Alabama, Jackson Hole, Wyoming, Perryville, Missouri, Salt Lake City, Utah, Savannah, Georgia, Wall, South Dakota and East Tennessee. There's also an international contribution to the series, Kilbirnie Scotland authored by Kitty McIntosh.

Sapphic Sweets Romantic short stories – Some sweet. Some with a little heat.

Individual Short Stories:

A Con Con – Mystery/Suspense

Before Dana – Erotica/Erotic Romance featuring Mel from the Morelville Mysteries Series

Crevice Chaos – Suspense/Thriller

Hazard Pay – Mystery/Suspense

Hunting You Down – Suspense

Midnight Slain in Georgia – Paranormal/Suspense/Thriller – features two characters from the Loving Blue in Red States short story, Savannah Georgia

Secret Masquerade – Erotic Suspense featuring Sheriff Mel from the Morelville Mysteries Series

Sundae Fun Day – Sweet romance

Treasure Hunted – Mystery – A Mel and Dana Short

<u>Waiting for You</u> - Romance